MW00958093

A
QUESTION
OF MAGIC

THE AGE OF MAGIC TRILOGY

A QUESTION OF MAGIC

Tom McGowen

LODESTAR BOOKS

Dutton   New York

Library of Congress Cataloging-in-Publication Data

McGowen, Tom.
  A question of magic / Tom McGowen.—1st ed.
    p.   cm.—(The Age of magic trilogy; bk. 3)
  "Lodestar books."
  Summary: When creatures from beyond the sky threaten to destroy the five intelligent races of ancient Earth and the mages of the land cannot agree on a plan, twelve-year-old Lithim and his father help to come up with a solution. Sequel to "The Magical Fellowship" and "A Trial of Magic."
  ISBN 0-525-67380-6
  [1. Fantasy.] I. Title. II. Series: McGowen, Tom. Age of magic trilogy; bk. 3.
PZ7.M16947Qu   1993
[Fic]—dc20   92-44112
                                                        CIP
                                                         AC

Published in the United States by Lodestar Books,
an affiliate of Dutton Children's Books,
a division of Penguin Books USA Inc.,
375 Hudson Street, New York, New York 10014

Published simultaneously in Canada
by McClelland & Stewart, Toronto

Editor: Rosemary Brosnan
Designer: Stanley S. Drate
Printed in the U.S.A. First Edition 10 9 8 7 6 5 4 3 2 1

for Brian
because he "couldn't wait to read it"

Prologue

It was a time that someday would be known as 30,000 B.C.—a time of shining ice and shimmering firelight, a time of wild, glorious greenness, a time of magic and enchantment.

Upon the northern part of the world squatted an enormous glacier, a gleaming mountain of ice that extended for thousands of miles. At its edge lay tundra, frozen flatland where only a few of the hardiest plants and animals could survive during a short "summer," when the temperature was barely above the freezing point. But as this flatland stretched southward, it grew warmer and wetter and was roamed by herds of musk-oxen and reindeer; packs of wolves; little clusters of shaggy, fur-coated rhinoceroses; and great herds of red-furred, curl-tusked mammoths. At length, the great cold plain came to a stop, halted by the wall of a vast black pine forest. And along the edge of this forest dwelt the slim, pale-eyed, silvery-haired Alfar, the ancient race of Elves, the first of Earth's thinking creatures.

The forest spread east, west, and south, changing character as it reached into warmer regions, with fir trees yielding to white-barked birches and gray-brown oaks, ashes, beeches, and rowans. It was an almost endless expanse of close-growing trees through which moved bears, herds of deer and shaggy forest bison, and scores of other creatures, big and small. Beneath parts of the forest stretched deep underground caverns, and these were the home of the Trolls, the second race of thinking beings. They were bulky, hulking, enormously strong creatures that came aboveground only by night, for the touch of sunlight was death to them.

In dry regions, grassy plains spread away from the forest, and there herds of wild horses ran, hunted by big saber-toothed cats and packs of wolves. Lakes and rivers abounded in fish, and the sky was often darkened by the passage of enormous flocks of birds. In places, the plains gave way to rolling hills, which were generally the territory of the small, yellow-eyed, foxlike Little People, the world's third thinking race. The hills gave way to stretches of mountains, the tops of which were the homes of the great, scaly, winged reptiles known as Dragons, the fourth thinking race.

In a part of the world east of the Great Forest and south of a region of hills and mountains lay a stronghold of the fifth thinking race. This was the Atlan Domain, a loosely bound federation of many small villages inhabited by humans who dressed in the skins of animals and made their tools of wood, stone, and bone. The Domain was ruled from a large island, Atlan Isle, which lay some distance off the west coast, in the green expanse of the Western Sea. Far to the east was another human domain, that of the Horse People, and across the Southern Sea was the kingdom of the Molo People.

Thus, the world was shared by five races of very different creatures that were all capable of thinking, conversing, and building. Each had its own goals, aspirations, and values. Because of great physical and mental differences among the races, they had little if any contact with one another, and some actively hated all those outside their own kind.

But all the races had one thing in common. Among each of them there were mages—individuals who could, to some extent, control destiny and environment by means of magic. And there came a time when the mages of all the world's races suddenly discovered that the planet upon which they lived faced the greatest and most terrifying of possible catastrophes.

It was the beginning of the time of year known as the Moon of First Snow, and indeed, the first snow of winter had been falling since noon over much of the Atlan Domain and the westernmost portion of the Great Forest. Billions of spinning white flakes had steadily piled up on every projecting tree branch and patch of ground where they could settle, and now the forest was a lacy panorama of gray, green, and white that glinted and gleamed to match the twinkle of stars in the cold black night sky.

Four Trolls were plodding through this part of the forest, heading westward. They were gray-skinned, immensely burly creatures, a head shorter than an average-size human but nearly three times as broad, with arms and legs as thick as small tree trunks. Between large, pale eyes set wide apart on each face jutted an enormously long, thick nose, beneath which was a thin-

5

lipped-mouth. Their ears were large and sharply pointed, and they twitched constantly, picking up the tiniest of sounds.

They moved in single file along a narrow trail that wound among the trees. The one in the lead was a powerful young warrior hefting a club made from a gnarled, stone-hard tree root, and the one at the rear was also a sturdy warrior, who was dragging along behind him a wooden sledge piled high with what appeared to be a bundle of furs. These two were clad only in trouserlike garments made of animal skin and were barefoot, for Trolls were virtually impervious to cold. The two in the middle, however, were wrapped in cloaks of bearskin, but these were symbols of rank rather than garments for warmth. Because of them, any Troll seeing these two would instantly recognize that they were High Wizards.

"This is the seventeenth night of our journey, oh Gwolchmig," rumbled one of the wizards, breaking a long period of silence. "I judge we must be within no more than four nights of this cursed human community we seek. Do you agree?"

"We should be out of these woods before the Eye of Day next peers over the world's edge," the one called Gwolchmig answered. "I judge that we shall then have three more full nights of travel, and midway through the fourth night we shall reach the human place called Soonchen."

The other gave a grunt of satisfaction, then seemed to reflect upon something for a time. "Trolls and humans have been deadly enemies for generations," he mused. "Never in my life did I once think I would be going into a human community to mingle with the creatures. It seems unnatural!"

"These are unnatural times, oh Kulglitch," Gwolchmig pointed out with unmistakable teasing in his tone. "After all, the world has never before faced doom as it now does, and that tends to make things somewhat unnatural."

Kulglitch's huge chest swelled in a sigh, and with his fingers he made a gesture that corresponded to a human's nod of agreement. Gwolchmig was referring to the horrifying danger that threatened the world, the danger that mages had named the Earthdoom. It did, indeed, make everything seem unnatural, for it threatened nothing less than the destruction of the earth.

Kulglitch remembered with painful clarity how he had first become aware of the Earthdoom. It had been at the beginning of the year, eight moons ago in the springtime, on the day when all the world's mages cast a Spell of Foreseeing to learn what the future held. Much of the Foreseeing had dealt with commonplace events, such as a wetter-than-usual summer and an early autumn. But then Kulglitch had been amazed to see that the Foreseeing was indicating that some kind of unknown creatures, in peculiar vessels, were journeying toward the earth from out of the great darkness beyond the stars, a thing that seemed absolutely impossible. Kulglitch's amazement had turned into shocked horror as the Foreseeing went on to reveal that when the creatures arrived, they were going to do things that would sear the world's lands with fire and explosions, boil the seas and lakes into steam, fill the air with poisonous smoke and vapors, and wipe out most life. What these creatures were and why they would do this was a mystery, but that the world faced destruction was agonizingly clear.

Kulglitch recalled, rather ruefully, that his reaction to what the Foreseeing had shown had simply been enraged hopelessness, with no thought of trying to do anything. But one mage—none other than the elderly High Wizard Gwolchmig, plodding along in front of him this very moment—*had* determined to do something. Gwolchmig had discerned a tiny gleam of hope in the Foreseeing, a hint that there might be a way to lessen, or perhaps even prevent, the Earthdoom if the mages of all the world's thinking races would band together and weld their powers into a single great weapon of magic with which to fight the creatures from the stars when they arrived. Such a thing seemed almost impossible, for the races had never cooperated in any way. The Dragons stayed remote and enigmatic; the Alfar were aloof and apparently disdainful of other creatures; the Little People would do their earnest best to slaughter any member of another race that entered their territory; and, as Kulglitch had mentioned, humans and Trolls had been bitter enemies for generations. Nevertheless, Gwolchmig had set out to do what he could.

He had risked his life to make contact with a powerful human High Wizard, Mulng of the Atlan Domain. To his relief and exultation, Mulng had eagerly accepted the Troll's suggestion that the world's mages join forces to fight the Star Creatures, and while Gwolchmig had then gone to try to seek an alliance with the Alfar, Mulng and his twelve-year-old son Lithim, an apprentice magician, had set out on a dangerous quest to attempt to gain the cooperation of the Dragons. It had turned out that most mages were eager to cooperate with one another, for they all realized this offered the only possible hope for saving the world. Recently, word had come to the Trolls that mages of all the races were gathering in the human village of Soonchen, on the northern frontier of the Atlan Domain, to hold a great council and determine how to merge their powers to fight against the Earth-doom.

And this is why, reflected Kulglitch, I am tramping along after Gwolchmig, risking death if a beam of the Day's Eye should touch me, in order to go among creatures I was regarding as mortal enemies no more than eight moons ago. Indeed, these are most unnatural times!

As Gwolchmig had predicted, they emerged from the forest sometime before dawn. Immediately, they made preparations to spend the day hidden away from the sunlight. This entire journey would have been impossible if it hadn't been for a sort of artificial cave that Gwolchmig had invented—a large sheet of animal skins sewn closely together, which formed a dome-shaped tent when fitted over a framework of peeled saplings. It was this contrivance, rolled up in a compact bundle, that the warrior Vorchmulg was pulling along on the sledge; and now they unrolled it and fitted it over the framework. After setting a number of snares to catch animals for food, and after the mages had ringed the dome with spells of warding and protection, the four sealed themselves within. Thus, they spent the hours of daylight in safe darkness, sleeping Troll-fashion, sitting up with their heads bent over their chests.

When night fell, they emerged, repacked the tent, collected the creatures that had been caught in their snares, which served as a breakfast, and continued on their way. They were traveling over a broad plain now, and with their extremely keen noses and other senses, they were perfectly aware of prowling sabertooths and other creatures that, hungry or not, knew better than to attack four full-grown Trolls. Nevertheless, animals often hopefully trailed them for a time.

They crossed the plain for three nights without incident, and on the fourth night, again as Gwolchmig had predicted, they saw ahead of them the log walls of the human village of Soonchen. The village stood at the edge of a long, narrow lake, a collection of some sixty cabinlike dwellings enclosed within a wall of upright logs and surrounded by a moat. As they drew closer, the Trolls could see that the drawbridge over the moat was down and the big gate stood open, although a handful of guards was present outside it, collected around a bonfire. Gwolchmig ordered the two young warriors to erect the shelter, and he and Kulglitch continued on toward the village. "The humans will mostly all be deep in sleep at this time of night," Gwolchmig remarked, "but I will tell those humans at the gate to let the High Wizard Mulng know we have arrived, when he awakens. We will meet with him at the beginning of tomorrow's night."

As they neared the drawbridge, their sensitive noses suddenly began to twitch, and they both halted in consternation. "There is a stench of death and rot and evil magic here," declared Kulglitch. He snorted in disgust.

"Yes, something dreadful has happened in this place," acknowledged Gwolchmig. "I pray that all is well!" He peered toward the gate. "It seems to be. The guards do not appear to be expecting any sort of trouble. Well, let us go on. Perhaps we can find out what has happened."

They moved onto the drawbridge, which creaked under their weight. The human guards had become aware of them and were watching their approach in silence and with obvious tension. Gwolchmig halted, feeling that it might be wise to identify himself before getting into spear range. "I am the High Wizard Gwolchmig of the Northland Trolls. I come in peace, at the invitation of the High Wizard Mulng. I wish to give him a message."

To his relief, the warriors relaxed visibly, and one of them moved toward him. "The High Wizard Mulng is expecting you," said the man. "He is sleeping now, of course, but he has given us instructions that he was to be awakened when you arrived. I will bring him here."

"Ah, that will be well," said Gwolchmig. "We will wait." He and Kulglitch squatted where they were, and the warrior turned and hurried off into the dark ways of the village.

"Whatever happened here took place mainly outside the walls," remarked Kulglitch. "I sense that the village was attacked."

"That is how it seems to me, too," said Gwolchmig. "But I cannot understand who might have attacked it. All the races have agreed to cooperate with one another in the effort to prevent the Earthdoom, and all the old enmities have been set aside, or so I thought."

They fell silent. After some time had passed, they saw two figures, one a head shorter than the other, coming through the gate toward them. Gwolchmig was sure this was the human mage Mulng and his twelve-year-old son, Lithim, and was gratified that Mulng had seen fit to bring the young one with him, for had the man come by himself, Gwolchmig was not sure he would have recognized him—humans all looked alike to Trolls—and that would be embarrassing. But the presence of the smaller figure made it obvious who the bigger one was. "Hail, Mulng," rumbled Gwolchmig, not rising.

"Hail, Gwolchmig. It is good to see you again," said the man.

Gwolchmig indicated his companion. "This is the wizard Kulglitch, a highly respected mage among Trolls. We have come to represent our people in this great council of mages that is taking place—if it *is* still taking place." He eyed the human with curiosity mixed with concern. "What has happened here? It reeks of blood and battle and evil magic!"

Mulng nodded. "Indeed, there have been battle and spilt blood and the wielding of evil magic here," he said in grim tones. "We have faced death and horror!" He squatted to face them on a level. "Let me tell you all that has taken place."

2

"I know that Trolls cannot understand the ways of humans," said Mulng, eyeing the two burly, gray-skinned creatures who were regarding him with their pale, bulging eyes. "So, much of what I have to say may be unfathomable. But you see, from the very beginning of our effort to help prevent the Earthdoom, I, and my son, and many of the Atlan mages who joined our effort have had to face opposition, treachery, the threat of death, and hopelessness! Gwolchmig, when you departed from my dwelling after our meeting eight moons ago, Lithim and I set out for Atlan Isle to tell the Atlan High Chieftain of your plan for averting the Earthdoom. But when we reached the island, we found opposition ranged against us! The priestesses who control the Atlan religion, those known as the Daughters of the Mother, refused to believe what the Foreseeing had shown of the Earthdoom and the creatures from the stars. They insisted that the Earth Mother, the great goddess that we Atlans believe made all things and is the very world itself, would not allow such a catastrophe as the Earthdoom to happen. They had convinced the High Chieftain that other mages and I were simply seeking to gain power by frightening people with predictions of disaster. The Chieftain ordered that no mage was either to speak of the Earthdoom or have anything to do with your plan to avert it, at risk of death by execution for blasphemy and treason!"

He shrugged. "Well, I and some of the others determined to defy the Chieftain and the Daughters. Lithim and I and a sorceress named Natl sneaked away from Atlan Isle to go north and try to make contact with the Dragons in hope of gaining their cooperation in your plan. We headed for the mountains north of here, where I had heard the great Dragon mage Klo-gra-hwurg-ka-urgu-nga dwelt."

He smiled. "But as things turned out, it wasn't even I who found the Dragon mage. *I* got captured by the Little People on the way to the mountains. Fortunately, they didn't want me for food, but to my astonishment, simply wanted to let me know that they wished to join in the effort against the Earthdoom, which their mages, too, had foreseen. Meanwhile, Lithim and Natl managed to find the Dragon mage, and it was actually Lithim who discovered how to talk to him, by means of the Spell of Mind-Touch." He reached up and patted the boy's shoulder with obvious pride. "Not many mages are capable of that spell, as you well know, and Lithim is even able to perform it across unlimited distances."

Gwolchmig knew that the boy was an apprentice mage, and therefore had to have a certain amount of magical skill, but for an apprentice to be able to do the things Mulng said he had done was quite remarkable. The Troll swung his big head to look at the (to him) incredibly fragile human child. Actually, Lithim was a sturdily built boy, with dark, intelligent eyes, auburn hair, and a handsome oval face, but none of these things were apparent to the Troll's eyes. Gwolchmig had first seen the boy during that fateful meeting with Mulng eight moons ago, but had paid little attention to him then, except to note that he seemed to possess a fairly high amount of mage power for one so young. Now the Troll was startled to feel that the child's mage power had obviously increased tremendously since that time; it surrounded him like a vibrant, swirling cloak of energy, quite apparent to another mage.

"I offer you my respect," he told the boy. "You accomplished what many a full-grown mage would have been unable to do." It was really beneath the dignity of a Troll High Wizard to give such a compliment to a mere child, Troll or human, but Gwolchmig felt compelled to do so.

Lithim's face broke into a smile. "Thank you, High Wizard. It is good to see you again."

Gwolchmig turned back to Mulng. "So you two managed to gain the cooperation of both the Little People and the Dragons. Remarkably well done! What then?"

"Then we came here," said Mulng. "Unfortunately, we no sooner came through the gate than we were seized and accused of blasphemy and treason, at the instigation of the village priestesses. We faced execution!

"Luckily," he continued, "the Chieftain of this village believed in what we are trying to do and sided with us against the Daughters of the Mother and the High Chieftain. He made this village a sanctuary for the realm's magicians, so that they could gather here openly to hold council on how best to fight the Star Creatures, instead of having to work in secrecy, at risk of death. We managed to let many know of this and they came here from all over the realm. We began to organize the council.

"But the Daughters of the Mother had not given up. They tried to put Lithim under an enchantment, and they tried to kill me. They managed to communicate with the High Chieftain and told him what was happening here. He came with a war band of a hundred men, intent upon destroying the village and slaughtering all the mages who had gathered in it!"

"We probably could have dealt with the war band," Mulng said, "but something else happened that very nearly ended everything. We were joined about that time by an Alfar mage, Aglinnadorn, who came here because of your visit to the Alfar, Gwolchmig. She warned us of another Alfar mage who was opposed to her people's decision to join our efforts against the Earthdoom. This mage was determined to prevent us from working against the Earthdoom because he *wanted* it to happen—he believed that the Alfar would survive it and become the world's masters again, as they had once been long ago. So he fought against us. He took over the High Chieftain's war band and battled us with that and with the darkest of evil magic. That is why you sense blood and death and evil here, Gwolchmig. He nearly prevailed. He was finally beaten by the efforts of three brave and skillful mages who risked horrible death—the Alfar woman; a Dragon mage; and my son, Lithim."

Gwolchmig and Kulglitch both turned their heads sharply to look at the boy. It was surprising that Mulng would have let an apprentice, and his only son as well, be a main combatant in what had obviously been a vital and deadly trial of magic, but it was becoming clear that this human child was quite extraordinary. "There is a great tale here, I think," Gwolchmig said to Lithim, "and some night you must tell it to me."

He looked back at Mulng. "Indeed, you have had many troubles, and I am most relieved that you manged to overcome them. I hope they are truly over now."

"It seems so," Mulng told him. "The Alfar wizard is dead, the High Chieftain's war band is scattered and probably still fleeing, and the Daughters of the Mother can do nothing more against us."

"Then all is well," Gwolchmig rumbled in satisfaction. "The way is clear for the council to carry out its task."

Mulng hesitated, as if choosing his words. "I, too, thought that with all our enemies defeated, our problems would be over. But when we began to hold council at last, we quickly discovered a new problem we had not anticipated."

"What?" Gwolchmig blinked at him. "What was it?"

"As we began to discuss how to combat the Sky Creatures, we realized that we truly know nothing about them," said Mulng. "The Foreseeing showed that they were very different from any kind of living creature on our world. Do you recall how it seemed to indicate that they were formed partly of flesh and partly of some kind of smooth, shining *rock?* They are unnatural, and the problem is: How can we be sure that any of the things we think of to use against them will actually be effective against creatures so different from anything we know?"

The Trolls stared at him wtih dawning dismay. "In the early meetings of the council, many ideas were suggested," Mulng went on. "Someone urged that the Dragons simply fly up and burn the Sky Creatures with their Spell of Fire-Casting. But someone else pointed out that rock cannot be harmed by fire, and inasmuch as the creatures are part rock, using fire against them might be useless. Another mage suggested using Spells of Illusion to frighten them off, but we do not know if such creatures *can* be frightened, or if they would even be aware of illusions. There was another suggestion that we try to take over their minds with Thought Magic, as we can do with many birds and animals—but we do not know if Thought Magic would work upon creatures from beyond the stars." He leaned toward the two Trolls, gesturing with his hand to emphasize his words. "Do you see the terrible problem we have? We may have only one quick chance against these creatures. If we waste that chance by doing something that is of no use, we will be like a hunter who has thrown his last spear at an angry, charging bear and has misssed! Whatever we decide to do against them must be something that we are *sure* will be effective, but there is no way for us to *be* sure against such unnatural creatures whose way of life we know nothing of!" He slapped his leg angrily. "And so, in council we argue and debate and puzzle endlessly, and each day the time to the Earthdoom grows shorter!"

As he finished speaking, the two Trolls turned their heads and looked at each other, and it seemed to the boy Lithim as if they had both thought of something simultaneously. "It is well, indeed, that Kulglitch and I have come," said Gwolchmig slowly, "for we Trolls can offer a way to solve your problem—a way to be completely sure that what is done against the Sky Creatures will be effective."

Mulng stiffened. "What is it?" he cried out in a voice that throbbed with hope.

"I cannot say more now," Gwolchmig told him. "Kulglitch and I must discuss this first. But if you will call a meeting of the mage council for tomorrow night, after darkness has arisen, I will tell everyone."

Mulng stared at them, and Lithim could feel that his father was bubbling with questions. But after a moment, the man dipped his head in a nod. "Very well. Do you wish to stay in the village until then? You should be safe enough inside one of the dwellings during the time of sunlight."

"No, we shall stay outside," the Troll told him. "We have a kind of artificial cave within which we spend the times of brightness. The two warriors who accompanied us on our journey here have erected it in yon field." He gestured toward the darkness beyond the moat. Then he glanced upward. "Perhaps we had best go take shel-

19

ter in it now, for it will not be long until the Eye of Day appears."

He stood up, and Kulglitch and Mulng followed suit. "We shall join you in the village when darkness arises tomorrow night," Gwolchmig said. The man and boy watched as the two hulking figures turned and trudged back over the drawbridge, merging into the darkness.

"I hope to the Mother that what he has promised is true," Mulng commented. He raised his eyes to stare up into the star-glittering blackness of the night sky.

Four billion miles out in the darkness beyond that sky, the five immense spacecraft of the creatures whose name for their race meant "The Industrious Ones" were passing through the orbit of Pluto, the ninth planet of the solar system to which Earth also belongs.

In appearance, The Industrious Ones were quite unearthly. Their race had achieved advanced technology thousands of years before and had soon begun to control its own evolution. It had altered the genetic makeup of its members and combined electronic circuitry with living tissue, so that each Industrious One was now partly flesh and blood and partly metal (which the Earth mages had identified as "shiny rock") and other artificial substances. Their knowledge was far greater than that of humans, and their goals and purposes would have been unknowable to a human; yet, in some few ways, they were similar to humans. They had individual personalities, and so they could be curious, ambitious, acquisitive, and capable of differences of opinion with one another.

From the surface of Pluto, Earth was not even visible, but on the efficient vision instruments of the vessels it was a circle as large as the palm of a human hand. The instruments clearly showed the dark blue of its oceans and the brown of land masses, partially obscured by the white wisps and curls of cloud formations. The vessels would reach orbiting position around it in a matter of a little less than five months, Earth time, and all The Industrious Ones aboard the vessels were eager to take part in the great enterprise of extracting the resources of the small planet. That this would cause tremendous destruction and the annihilation of many living things did not trouble them. Their probes of Earth, sent there long before, had indicated that the small planet did not harbor any intelligent life, and The Industrious Ones had no concern about any other kind.

It had been pleasant to see Gwolchmig the Troll once again, thought Lithim, although he ruefully admitted to himself that he hadn't really been sure, at first, which of the two Trolls squatting by the gate the previous night *was* Gwolchmig. Trolls all looked alike to him, and he had seen Gwolchmig only once before, eight moons ago. However, once Gwolchmig had identified himself, Lithim had truly felt pleasure in knowing this was the same Troll who had come to his father's dwelling on that night back in the Moon of Budding Trees, with his great plan to save the world from the Earthdoom. It had been Gwolchmig's visit that had sent Lithim off on a wonder-filled journey, during which he had seen more of the world than he ever expected to, made new friends, and become part of the most important event in all of history. If it had not been for Gwolchmig's visit, mused the boy, I would probably still be in the Great Forest now, just waiting around for the

Earthdoom to come along and kill me before I've even seen thirteen summers.

He was seated cross-legged upon a fur robe spread out on the snowy ground of the village square of Soonchen. The village had been cloaked in night's darkness for some time, but instead of being quiet and asleep, as it would have been on most nights, it was ablaze with light and bustling with activity. In the square, which was the center of converging rows of dwellings, bonfires and numerous torches flared, painting with flickering orange light the fur-clad people thronging the area. Those around the edges of the square were residents of the village, standing in small family groups or clusters of neighbors. Their attention was directed inward, where a large number of persons were seated, forming a wide three-deep circle. These were the mages who had come to Soonchen from all parts of the Atlan Domain, and from places outside the Domain, to work out a plan for preventing the Earthdoom.

While most of those forming the ring of mages were human, some were not. The two Trolls, Gwolchmig and Kulglitch, sat stolidly among the humans, making Lithim think of a pair of bulky gray boulders poking up in a patch of slim birch saplings. In another part of the circle crouched a cluster of Little People: yellow-eyed, fox-faced creatures whose thin, shaggy bodies were no bigger than that of a human two-year-old. There was a single tall, slim person with ivory pale skin, silvery hair, and eyes like shining mirrors—an Alfar woman, the mage Alglinnadorn. And there was one nonhuman mage who would take part in the council but who was not physically present because his enormous bulk simply could not squeeze into the square. This was the Dragon Gra-kwo, who, since coming to Soonchen, had made his dwelling place in a sizable clearing within the small forest known as Darkwood, some distance north of the village.

When the great Dragon mage Klo-gra-hwurg-ka-urgu-nga had agreed to lead his fellow Dragon mages in cooperating with the mages of other races to avert the Earthdoom, he had sent young Gra-kwo back to Soonchen with Lithim and the other humans. Gra-kwo would be the Dragons' representative at the mage council Mulng hoped to arrange. On the journey back, Gra-kwo and Lithim had become close friends, and they had discovered that, whereas a few non-Dragon mages, such as Mulng and Alglinnadorn, could exchange mind-touch with Dragons face-to-face, Lithim was able to do it across unlimited distances, just as Dragons could. And so Gra-kwo would be able to take part in the council through Lithim. It would be the boy's task to keep the Dragon informed of what the mages in Soonchen had to say and to repeat Gra-kwo's comments and suggestions to them.

A mage council was a highly formal affair, based upon rules set down hundreds of years earlier. One person, generally the mage of highest ability and respect who was present, was chosen to conduct things, and he or she began by giving a short speech outlining the purpose of the council. Then, any mages who desired to speak raised their hands, and the leader designated a speaker by pointing. Because it was largely through Mulng's efforts that this council at Soonchen had been made possible, he had almost automatically been chosen its leader. He stood in the center of the ring of mages, leaning on his staff and glancing about to determine if all those who were to take part in the council had arrived and found a place within the circle. At length, he lifted his staff in a signal for silence, and the hum of voices of those in the circle and in the watching crowd quickly died away. Mulng spoke.

"I have good tidings," he announced. "We have spent days trying to solve the problem of how to prevent the enemy Sky Creatures from bringing about the Earth-doom when they come, but we could not be sure that any of our ideas would actually work. Well, it now seems that there may be a way for us to *be* sure. As you know, we have been joined by the High Wizards Gwolchmig and Kulglitch of the Trolls. High Wizard Gwolchmig has told me that the Trolls may have a way of solving our problem!" He pointed toward the two bulky gray figures. "High Wizard Gwolchmig, I ask you to tell this council what it is that the Trolls can do to help us."

Ponderously, Gwolchmig got to his feet. The eyes of every person in the Soonchen village square were upon him, and the silence was so deep that the crackling of the fires and torches as their flames snapped in the winter wind was as loud as handclaps.

"Within the deepest, most remote caverns of the realm of Northland Trolls," said Gwolchmig, "there dwells one who is called by us the Undying One, for she has been known to many generations of Trolls back through our history. She herself is not a Troll; she is, we think, the last living member of a race of creatures that once lived in the underground regions where we Trolls now make our home. But she dwells far from us, in a cavern where vapors ooze up out of the very depths of earth. She is a mage, and she has one very special magical ability—when asked a question, she will give an answer that is always correct. If we were to ask her exactly what to do to prevent the Earthdoom, she could tell us."

A sound like a faint sigh whispered among the circle of seated mages when the Troll finished speaking, and Lithim ruefully recognized it as the sound of disappointment. The mages had listened hopefully for a real solution to their problem, and this talk of an undying oracle was not what they had wanted to hear. There were oracles and prophets among humans, too, but they were invariably tricksters and shams, and there was no reason to believe that this oracle the Trolls had such faith in would be any different.

With a mental sigh of disappointment of his own, Lithim channeled his thoughts along the path that brought him into mind-touch with the Dragon in the distant forest, and he repeated the Troll's words. "What do you think of this, Gra-kwo?" he questioned.

In a moment, Gra-kwo's thoughts came flooding into his mind, oddly patterned and phrased, but clearly understandable.

"This one senses doubt in you, Lith-im, but this one feels we should withhold judgment until more is learned."

Lithim smiled. That was the way of Dragons, of course; they never made up their minds in a hurry, preferring to give considerable thought to things. It was apparent to Lithim that his father, too, was willing to suspend judgment until he learned more, for he asked Gwolchmig, "Do your people question this Undying One often?"

"No more than absolutely necessary," said the Troll, who had remained standing. "Trolls have seen fit to question Gurda, the Undying One, only twice in the last one hundred years, and that was for the purpose of getting answers to questions that affected their very survival. You see, it is not an easy thing to do. There are many dangers, even for Trolls, in making the journey through the caverns to where she dwells. And there is a very great price that must be paid for the asking of the question."

"What price?" asked Mulng.

"I will not speak of that now. But if it is the wish of the council, I will make the journey and ask the question, so that we may learn exactly what we must do about the Sky Creatures." Lithim noticed that as Gwolchmig said this, Kulglitch looked at him with an expression that seemed to the boy to be one of concern.

"The council must decide," stated Mulng and glanced about. A number of hands shot up.

The mage Mulng pointed to was the big, red-faced, white-haired High Wizard Gling, from Atlan Isle. "High Wizard Gwolchmig," he said respectfully, facing the Troll, "is there—uh—any doubt at all in your mind about the absolute correctness of what this Gurda told those who questioned her? Was she at all vague in her answers, or were they clear and precise? Did she ever actually *predict* something that really occurred?"

Gwolchmig's face twisted in the grimace that passed for a smile among Trolls. "You think, perhaps, that we

27

poor Trolls have been taken in by a false oracle? Well, let me tell you of what happened when she was last questioned, in the generation of the mother of my mother's mother. It was a time of terrible unrest of the earth, when tremors and shakings were taking place. A severe tremor had caused a cave-in of an empty cavern not far from the main dwelling cavern of my people, and the clan leaders were fearful that such a thing might occur there as well. They made the decision to consult Gurda to determine if the clans were safe. She told them to abandon their cavern, for it would be destroyed by the earth's shakings. They did so, and two nights after the last Troll had left, a mighty quake caused the cavern's ceiling to fall. Thousands of Trolls would have been killed and injured but for Gurda's prediction. And I tell you that within all our history of her, there is no record that she ever answered a question wrongly!"

"Well," said Gling, fingering his chin thoughtfully, "perhaps we should try this, then."

"High Wizard Mulng!" Alglinnadorn, the Alfar mage, had risen to her feet and was anxiously indicating that she wished to speak. Mulng pointed to her.

"It is essential that we indeed send High Wizard Gwolchmig to ask this question," she declared. "We Alfar know something of this Undying One's race, but we did not know any of them still survived, much less one that is a mage. Do you all realize what this means?" She peered about at the faces turned toward her. "She is the last mage—the only mage—of one of the world's thinking races. Remember what the Foreseeing revealed: that the mages of *all* the world's thinking races must participate in the effort to prevent the Earthdoom. Thus, to fulfill the Foreseeing, *she* must participate, or else the effort will surely fail! By answering the question that the High Wizard Gwolchmig puts to her, she will be doing her part, and the Foreseeing will be fulfilled!"

An excited hum of voices arose. Lithim quickly relayed the Alfar's words to Gra-kwo, and the Dragon's return thoughts came rushing into his mind. *"She is right, Lith-im! The Troll must go to this mage and ask her the question!"*

"Father," said Lithim from where he sat near Mulng's feet, within the center of the circle of mages, "Gra-kwo agrees with Alglinnadorn."

"So do I," said Mulng. He lifted his staff for silence. "Mages," he called in a ringing voice, "the council must vote on this matter. But I tell you that I agree with the mage Alglinnadorn, and so does the Dragon mage Gra-kwo. I think it is the greatest good fortune that we learned of this, and I give thanks to the Mother! I now ask all who would have High Wizard Gwolchmig go and question this oracle to raise their hands."

Hands went up, some instantly, some more hesitantly, but there was a clear majority.

"Very well," said Mulng. "Gwolchmig shall go, then." He looked toward the Troll. "How long will the journey take?"

"From here to the domain of my people, twenty-one nights," replied Gwolchmig. "Then, to reach the cavern of the Undying One, about three more nights."

Mulng was taken aback. "Why, that would mean twenty-four days going there and twenty-four more coming back here to bring us the answer," he exclaimed. "That's nearly two whole moons, and we have less than five moons before the Sky Creatures arrive. That leaves us little time to do whatever the oracle tells you must be done!"

Lithim felt his heart leap. "Father," he cried, "I know how we can cut those forty-eight days in half. I can go with Gwolchmig, and when he gets the oracle's answer, I can tell it to Gra-kwo at once, and then he can fly here from his forest and tell you or one of the others who can communicate with him at close range. You'll have the answer in twenty-four days instead of forty-eight."

Mulng had whirled to stare down at him. Then the man knelt, putting his mouth close to the boy's ear. "No, Lithim," he said in a low voice that only his son could hear. "I can't let you go off into danger again. Your life was at risk when you went to make contact with the Dragon mage, and it was at even greater risk when you went with Alglinnadorn to do magical combat against the Alfar wizard. I can't let you risk your life a third time, against dangers that even the Trolls seem to fear!"

"Your son's suggestion has great merit, Mulng," called Gwolchmig. "It will be well to gain those twenty-four days and nights of time, for who knows what lengthy labors Gurda may tell us we must do? I know that you fear for him, but I pledge to you that if he makes the journey with me, I will look after his safety as if he were a child of my own. When we set out for the Undying One's cavern, I will take along a war band of proven Troll warriors to guard and protect him, and I pledge they will give up their lives, if necessary, to keep him safe!"

Mulng said nothing, but continued to look at Lithim with anxious eyes. "Father," said Lithim, speaking in low tones as the man had, "remember what I told you when I went to help Alglinnadorn fight the Alfar wizard? It didn't *matter* that I was going into danger because I am in danger all the time already from the Earthdoom! If I simply try to stay safe now, and the Earthdoom can't be stopped, I'll probably be dead in four more moons. But by risking danger to do something that may help prevent the Earthdoom from happening, I may be saving my life! Going with Gwolchmig gives me a chance to help myself and everyone else. I must do it, Father."

"Mulng," a thin, quavering voice called out suddenly. It was the elderly mage of the Little People, Neomah. "Let the young one do this thing. It is his destiny. I felt from the moment I first saw him and sensed his growing power that he was *born* for this time of trouble. I tell you that he will be unharmed, for he still has a great part to play in averting the Earthdoom."

Moments passed; then Lithim saw Mulng shake himself slightly and knew that his father had come to a decision. "Very well," said Mulng, rising to his feet and looking around the circle of silent mages, whose eyes were all fixed upon him. "Lithim shall accompany the High Wizard Gwolchmig to the abode of the Undying One. But I urge the members of this council to select a new leader if they plan to continue their discussions. Alglinnadorn, I charge you to be ready to take the message from Gra-kwo when he brings it, for I will not be here. This time when my son risks his life, *I* am going to be with him!"

The hardest part of the journey to the domain of the Trolls, it seemed to Lithim when they started out, was the necessity of having to sleep during the day. The two humans and four Trolls traveled by night, of course, with the Trolls erecting their big animal-hide tent and retiring into it well before sunup each morning. They had invited Lithim and Mulng to join them in the tent, but the man and boy had felt they would be less crowded and more comfortable sleeping outside. However, trying to fall asleep when the sun was just rising and the sky growing ever brighter was difficult for the first few days, no matter how fatigued they were from a night of steady walking. But their bodies eventually adjusted to the change, and sleep came as easily with the sunrise as it normally did with sunset and darkness.

The first three nights they had tramped eastward across the plain, but midway through the fourth night they had reached the outskirts of the Great Forest. Entering it was like a homecoming for Lithim, for he had spent almost the entire twelve years of his life living in this forest with his father. He had been born in the big community of Atlan Dis, on Atlan Isle, but his mother had died soon after giving him birth, and sometime later his father had taken him to the Northland Forest to dwell. For Mulng had sensed strong mage power in the boy, and he knew that the best way to develop mage talent to its fullest was to keep the child living apart from others, under dangerous conditions that would help accelerate his abilities. Mulng had chosen to rear Lithim in the isolation of the forest, among the dangers of wild animals and, at that time, human-hating Trolls. So Lithim had grown up in this world of endless trunks, limbs, and leaves and was happy to visit it again.

Night after night they tramped along. Their food consisted mainly of small animals and birds that were caught in snares placed around the campsite each sleep period. These creatures were prepared, generally by roasting or stewing, by one of the Troll warriors. To Lithim's surprise, he was an exceptionally skillfull cook who flavored his dishes with certain herbs, berries, and roots he gathered up as he plodded along each night. However, Troll tastes were somewhat different from those of humans, and Lithim generally found the dishes somewhat pungent and tangy.

Trolls were far more taciturn and less communicative than humans, speaking only when necessary. Lithim had tried to draw Gwolchmig into conversation, but met with only limited success. The boy had asked the Troll about his comment that there were many dangers in the deep caverns near the Troll domains, which even Trolls feared. Lithim had asked what sorts of dangers he meant.

"Many dangerous creatures stalk and creep and crawl through the depths of the world," Gwolchmig had told him, "but the chief danger is from worms."

"Worms?" Lithim exclaimed, his voice expressing incredulity.

"Not the soft little mud-eating worms you know of," said the Troll, regarding the boy with his pale eyes. "These worms are larger than your Dragon friend. Their bodies are armored, and they are predators." He then turned away and became silent, leaving Lithim with a great deal to think about. Mulng caught his son's eye and made a wry grimace that seemed to say, "What have we gotten ourselves into now?"

After some sixteen nights of travel through the forest, they began to encounter moss-covered boulders poking up out of the ground, sometimes with the roots of great trees clutching them like a gnarly hand. It soon became obvious that this part of the forest had once been a rocky mountainside that had been worn down by millenia of wind and rain and covered over with a layer of soil out of which segments, slabs, and shelves of rock protruded here and there. On the seventeenth night, the travelers came upon the wide, dark mouth of a cave, before which a pair of Troll warriors were standing guard. The guards bowed to the two Troll wizards but stared and shifted nervously as the human man and boy passed by them, following Gwolchmig and Kulglitch into the cave.

"You are the first humans to ever enter these caverns by invitation, rather than as bound, guarded prisoners," remarked Kulglitch. "I'm afraid it is rather upsetting to the portal guards. They have regarded humans as enemies since they were born." Lithim nodded, remembering how the human guards had stared uncomfortably at the two Trolls as they squatted before the north gate of the village on the night they had arrived. He could not help but think again, as he often had during the past eight moons, that the fear of the Earthdoom was actually doing some good. It was forcing a lot of the old enmities to be reconsidered.

The cave entrance led into a rocky tunnel that angled downward. Like most nocturnal creatures, Trolls could see in the darkness of a night-shrouded forest or plain because their eyes were capable of gathering in the faintest gleams of moonlight and starlight and reflecting them back to illuminate the surroundings. But there was no moonlight or starlight underground, so Troll eyes were as useless there as human eyes; and the Trolls used torches, placed in clefts in the rock walls at intervals of every forty paces or so, to light the way through the tunnel. The descent became quite steep, but crude steps had been hacked into the stone floor, which made the going easier. There were a great many steps, and almost subconsciously Lithim began to count them. When he reached 243, the ground became level, and the two humans and four Trolls passed through an archway formed of morticed blocks of stone. The archway led into an enormous cavern, the floor of which was well lit by torches, but the roof of which was so high and the length so great that both the cavern's ceiling and end were lost in darkness. It was the floor of the cavern that captured the attention of Lithim and his father, however, for upon it, lit by torches stuck into every niche and cranny, stood a Troll city.

The rock floor of the cavern was studded with hundreds of stalagmites: tall cones of gray limestone, thick as tree trunks, which the Trolls had used as corner posts and columns for their dwellings. The walls of the dwellings were formed of chunks of rock obviously hewn from the walls of the cavern itself, piled atop one another in rows stretching from one stalagmite to the next one, creating enclosures that were triangular, squarish, five-sided, or six-sided, depending upon the number of stalagmites forming their corners. Within these enclosures groups of Trolls slept, ate their meals, and spent much of their time, and there was a gray, solid, stolid chunkiness about the dwellings that seemed to suggest the Trolls themselves, thought Lithim.

When the boy and his father entered the community, following their four Troll companions, the narrow, tunnel-like paths winding in and out among the stretches of stone wall on each side seemed to Lithim more like a maze than the streets of a community. They encountered many Trolls moving up and down these paths, but instead of stopping to stare and collect into crowds as humans might have done, the burly gray creatures simply cast curious sidelong glances at the two humans and continued to shamble on their way. Lithim was amused, however, when several small-sized Trolls, obviously children, made horrible faces at him as he passed them by.

After some time, Gwolchmig and the other Trolls halted before the entrance to a dwelling that looked no different from any of the others. The old wizard said something in the Troll language to the two warriors, who bowed and departed. Gwolchmig turned to the humans.

"This is the dwelling of my clanbrothers," he told them. "I invite you and the High Wizard Kulglitch to stay here with me until we commence our expedition to the cavern of the Undying One." He stepped aside and gestured for them to enter. Kulglitch strode through the portal, and Mulng and Lithim hastened to follow.

Once inside, Lithim could see, in the near darkness, that the enclosure was divided into a number of rock-walled cubicles arranged around a larger central area, where a log fire glowed within a ring of large stones. Several Trolls were squatting around the fire, sipping some fluid out of tiny stone cups. At the entrance of the humans, their faces registered unmistakable shock and surprise. Gwolchmig quickly spoke to them and they relaxed, although they continued to stare.

"These are my clanbrothers," Gwolchmig explained. "I have told them why you are here, and they accept your presence as my guests. I will not bother to give you their names, nor to give yours to them, for you will not stay here more than one sleep-time, and you will probably never see them again after that. So names do not matter." He indicated a nearby cubicle. "It is nearly sleep-time now. You may use that area as your sleeping place. I will wake you and see that you are fed. We shall begin the rest of our journey soon after that."

Mulng silently bowed and Lithim quickly followed his example. They turned away and entered the tiny room that was to be their sleeping quarters for the "night," which would actually be day in the world above. How can they keep such things straight, wondered Lithim, when it is always dark everywhere in the domain of Trolls?

Another thought struck him as he and Mulng settled themselves among the piles of furs spread over the stone floor. "Father, Gwolchmig called this the dwelling of his clanbrothers, and those Trolls by the fire are all males. Is this place only for Troll *men?*"

The cubicle, cut off from the glow of the firelight by a section of wall, was quite dark and Lithim could not see his father's face, but something in the voice made him feel that Mulng was smiling. "Yes, Trolls do not live in families as humans do. The males and females of each clan live in separate dwellings from one another. The boy children live in the women's dwelling with their mothers until they reach a certain age, when they go to the males' dwelling and live there from then on."

"Don't they *ever* go back for visits?" wondered the boy.

"Males never go back to the female dwelling and females never go into a male dwelling," Mulng told him, "but each clan has a special place where male and female clan members can go to meet one another and visit."

"We're all so different," marveled Lithim. "Each human family lives in its own little dwelling; whole groups of Little People families live all together in big earth lodges; and here, males and females live apart in their own dwellings and there are no families. And Dragons not only have no families, they don't even live together; every Dragon lives by itself from the time it hatches." Speaking of Dragons made him think of Gra-kwo, and he reached out with mind-touch, knowing that even though it was barely sunrise aboveground, the Dragon, who slept very little, would probably be awake. "Gra-kwo, we have reached the domain of the Trolls. We are in their underground village."

They were many hundreds of thousands of paces apart, Lithim knew, but the Dragon's thoughts came to him as clearly as if the two of them were only at arm's length. "*Ah, then soon you will meet/contact/encounter the one whom the Trolls believe can give us the undoubted answer on how to deal with the Sky Creatures. This one is eager to learn that answer. When this one receives it from you, this one will fly at once to the human community to convey/carry/bring it to the mages there.*"

"We will be starting out on our journey to the oracle tomorrow," Lithim told him. "That will be tonight for you, of course; everything is turned around when you're with Trolls! But anyway, I guess it will take several days—whole days, I mean—to get there, if everything goes well and we don't run into any trouble. Gwolchmig says there are dangerous things down here, such as giant worms bigger than Dragons."

"*Indeed?*" There was alarm in Gra-kwo's thought

patterns. *"This one wishes he could be there in case you need him, Lith-im. This one feels sure that no worm could be a match for/an equal of/a threat to one of the Beautiful People, no matter how big it might be!"*

"I wish you could be here, too," the boy assured him. "But I'm sure we'll be all right. There will be plenty of Trolls to look after us." He found himself yawning. "I'm getting sleepy. Good night, Gra-kwo. I hope that the next time I contact you it will be to give you the answer we've gotten from the oracle."

"This one shares that hope, Lith-im. Good night. And may that Mother you worship watch over you on your journey."

Lithim was awakened by his father. "Time to be up and about, Lith," said the man. "Gwolchmig wants to get started as soon as we have something to eat."

It was impossible to tell how long he had slept, for the tiny room was as dark as it had been the "night" before, but Lithim felt refreshed and ready for breakfast. He fumbled in the darkness for his boots and jacket, which he had removed before going to sleep; donned them; picked up his mage staff; and followed Mulng out into the main room of the clan house. He looked about hopefully for a vessel of water so that he might wash his face, but apparently Trolls did not follow such a practice. There were no washing materials in sight. The fire within the ring of stones had been built up, and there were several more Trolls seated around it than there had been, Gwolchmig and Kulglitch among them. Most of them had what appeared to be large wooden bowls in their hands, from which they were taking frequent noisy sips. At the sight of the humans, Gwolchmig silently extended two such bowls to them, and accepting one, Lithim saw that it contained a large handful of round mushroom heads in a thick brown broth.

He sat down beside his father, noticing as he did so that while he and Mulng sat cross-legged, as most humans always did, the Trolls all sat with their legs stretched straight out in front of them. He had to repress a giggle at the sight of so many huge, flat-bottomed feet and lumpy toes. The Trolls ate in silence, except for the sounds of their slurps, pointedly ignoring the humans. Lithim found the mushroom broth to be pungently spiced in Troll style, but it was warm and filling and he gobbled it up gratefully.

Finishing, he put the bowl down beside him on the stone floor, as all the Trolls seemed to be doing when they were through, and looked around. At that moment a Troll carrying a stone-tipped spear came into the enclosure from outside and said something in a low voice to Gwolchmig. The wizard made a brief reply, then looked across the fire toward Lithim and his father. "All is ready," he said, and he and Kulglitch rose to their feet.

Mulng did likewise, and Lithim jumped up beside him. Gwolchmig said a few words to his clanbrothers seated around the fire. They responded loudly in unison with a single word and bowed their heads to him. Lithim had the feeling that they were showing great honor to the old Troll wizard. Gwolchmig turned and paced toward the entrance, followed by Kulglitch and the two humans.

Outside, the narrow, tunnel-like "street" that ran past the dwelling was filled with Trolls, at least a dozen of them, all armed with spears and many also bearing animal-skin bags and bundles of thick tree branches for use as torches. All these Trolls, Lithim decided, were the war band that Gwolchmig had promised would accompany them on their journey, mainly to safeguard Lithim himself. Even though Gwolchmig's reference to giant worms had caused Lithim some misgivings, the sight of all these immensely strong warriors was reassuring.

Gwolchmig and Kulglitch conferred for a few moments with several of the warriors; then Gwolchmig glanced toward the two humans. "We depart now for the place of the Undying One," he informed them, and turning, strode off with Kulglitch at his side. The warriors began to trail after, and Lithim and Mulng quickly joined in with them.

The procession of mages and warriors wound through the narrow streets of the Troll community, which was well lit by many torches set in cracks and niches in the walls of dwellings. But after a time, the procession turned down a short street lit by only a single torch, and Lithim saw that nothing but unbroken blackness lay beyond the street's end. They had reached the city's outskirts. Several of the Troll warriors poked the tips of tree branches into the flame of the solitary torch, and when the branches began to flare, becoming torches themselves, the Trolls holding them moved out to the front and sides of the column proceeding down the street. Lithim knew that with nothing more than the light of those three torches the Trolls could see clearly for many dozens of paces all around them. But now that he and his father were beyond the faint glow of torchlight that had illuminated the Troll community, the darkness was so intense for their human eyes that even though they were side by side and close together, they could not see each other. Almost instinctively, they reached out, groping, and joined hands so that they would not become separated.

It was an eerie and unpleasant experience to move through such total darkness, with only three flickering splotches of torchlight to mark the way to go. Lithim had always believed that a forest at night was the darkest of all places, but now he realized that there was far more light aboveground at night, from moon and stars, than he had ever really noticed. But no light at all, from stars, moon, or even sun, reached this far down into the earth. This was a realm of complete blackness. Lithim recalled Gwolchmig's comment that many dangerous creatures stalked and crept and crawled through these black caverns, and a sudden shiver twisted his spine. He and his father would be completely helpless against such creatures, which were undoubtedly well equipped to live in this darkness, with incredibly good smell and hearing and probably other senses as well, to help them locate their prey. He knew that he and Mulng were in the center of a Troll war band, with warriors all around them to protect them; but even so, he could not refrain from walking with hunched shoulders and drawn-in neck, in a feeble effort to protect himself against anything that might come leaping, lurching, or slithering out of the blackness that engulfed him on all sides.

To try to forget his fears, the boy searched his mind for something to talk about. He recalled the remark Gwolchmig had made when he had spoken to the council about the Undying One: that she required a large payment of some kind for answering questions. "Father," he said, "do you suppose that some of the Troll warriors are carrying the oracle's payment with them? I wonder what it could be." He kept his voice at a whisper, fearing that a louder sound would echo through the cavern and perhaps attract something's attention.

"I have wondered about that myself," said Mulng's voice beside him. Mulng, too, spoke in low tones. "The Trolls don't use gold nuggets to pay for things as we do, but even if they did, I can't imagine what use gold would be to a creature that apparently lives alone in a cave full of vapors! Perhaps the Trolls pay her with food. Some of the warriors are carrying bags full of foodstuff. I'll ask Gwolchmig about it when I get a chance."

"Ask me about what?" said the voice of Gwolchmig, suddenly coming out of the darkness just ahead of them, causing Lithim to jump slightly.

"Why, about the price that must be paid to your oracle for answering our question," said Mulng. "You told us it was a high price, but you did not tell us what it was. Perhaps it is something we could help pay."

"No." The word was spoken with firmness. "It is not your concern. Do not trouble yourselves about it."

He said nothing more. Lithim trudged on, his mind full of questions. The matter of the oracle's payment had become a mystery.

The march through darkness began to take on an

almost dreamlike quality. The blackness was so intense that the boy's mind seemed to try to compensate for it, and Lithim thought he could see patches of dark, sullen colors beginning to form all around him; the black-red of drying blood, the black-green of a pine forest seen from a distance, the blue-black of an early night sky. He also felt as if he were drifting into slumber even as he continued to walk. He shook his head vigorously to wake himself up and squeezed his mage staff with a tighter grip. Even so, with the blackness lulling him, he soon slipped into an almost trancelike state, half awake and half dreaming.

An unknown time later, he was suddenly jarred into full wakefulness by the sound of Gwolchmig's voice. "We will halt now," said the Troll loudly. Lithim stumbled to a stop and might have fallen, save that he was still clutching his father's hand. Yawning, he became aware that he was ravenously hungry.

The glows of the three torches began to converge inward toward one another as the Trolls holding them moved in from their places at the front and on the flanks to join the main group. The torches were piled together on the ground to provide a tiny campfire, and the Trolls and two humans gathered closely around it. One of the Trolls began handing out chunks of dried meat from a leathern bag, and Lithim shortly found himself munching away and speculating as to whether this was a "noontime" meal or an "evening" one, for he had no idea how long they had been traveling. He suspected it was probably a luncheon rather than a supper, however.

Abruptly he became aware that the Troll seated next

to him, on the opposite side from his father, was Kul-glitch, clearly visible in the glow of the campfire. Al-though most Trolls still looked alike to the boy, he had become sufficiently familiar with the facial characteristics of Gwolchmig and Kulglitch to be able to recognize them. It occurred to him that perhaps Kulglitch would be willing to explain the little mystery that Lithim had been turning over in his mind.

"High Wizard Kulglitch," he said respectfully, "do you know how High Wizard Gwolchmig intends to pay the Undying One?"

Kulglitch paused in his chewing and looked at the boy for a long moment. "With his life," he said and resumed his jaw movements.

Lithim felt stunned, not at all sure he had understood correctly. "You mean he must *die* for some reason if he asks the question?"

"That is the payment Gurda requires," said Kulglitch. "She needs servants to care for her wants, but ordinary Trolls would be useless to her because they would even-tually die, while she lives on. So, as payment for an-swering a question, Gurda causes a Troll to die, then brings him back to a kind of undying life to be her servant from then on. Such a Troll is mindless and can do only whatever Gurda tells him to do."

"Did you hear that, Father?" Lithim exclaimed.

"Yes," said Mulng, his tone grim. "Had I known this, I would never have agreed to let him do it. We must stop him!"

"You cannot," declared Kulglitch. "You have no right to tell Gwolchmig what he can or cannot do, and he is determined to do this. If the question of how to fight the Sky Creatures is never answered, then the Earthdoom will almost surely take place and most living things will die, Gwolchmig among them. But by dying now to get the answer, he can save the others. He is willing to do this."

He said no more, and both Lithim and Mulng were silent, feeling there was little or nothing they could say. Lithim felt tears gathering as he considered the bravery of the hulking, misshapen old Troll mage. While the boy understood quite well that Gwolchmig was mainly concerned with trying to save his own people, the Trolls, his action would also save Lithim, and Lithim felt humbled by that.

Shortly, the Trolls began to make ready to resume the journey. Three new torches were set ablaze from the embers of the campfire, and once again the march through darkness began, with the glow of the torches at the front and on the flanks to mark the way. Lithim tramped along with his mind in turmoil over the shocking news about Gwolchmig. He was sincerely saddened by the thought of the Troll's death, but he was full of admiration for Gwolchmig's courage and determination and wondered if he would be capable of making such a sacrifice as Gwolchmig was prepared to make. It was true that Lithim had risked his life several times for the effort against the Earthdoom, but he had done so with knowledge that there was a chance he would survive, whereas Gwolchmig had resigned himself to certain death.

"I wish he did not have to do it," he murmured,

knowing that his father, walking beside him, would understand what he spoke of.

"So do I," said Mulng softly.

When the march finally halted again, a seemingly interminable time later, Lithim knew that it was now an "evening" halt, which would be devoted to a period of sleep. And indeed, after another meal of cold dried meat, most of the Trolls began composing themselves for sleep around the fire, as did Lithim and Mulng. At three widespread points outside the circle of sleepers, Troll warriors kept watch, staring out into the dark distance of the cavern, their pointed ears twitching to pick up the smallest of sounds.

Lithim was awakened by the activity of the Troll warriors as they prepared for the second "day" of the journey. Breakfast was more of the cold dried meat, washed down by swigs of water from leather bags, and Lithim suspected this was what he would be eating for the remaining two days of the march to the Undying One's cavern and the three-day journey back to the Troll community. It did not matter greatly to him; after all, the important thing was to reach the oracle and have the question answered, and food was merely a means of keeping up strength in order to get that done.

Once again the boy and his father held hands as they tramped through the blackness, so that they wouldn't lose contact with each other and have no one to talk to. Actually, they did very little talking, for the darkness had a subduing, depressing effect, especially since they were now aware that each step of the journey was bringing Gwolchmig closer to his death.

After a time, Lithim noticed that the three torches lighting the expedition's way were much closer together than they had been, and it also seemed to him that the Trolls were bunched more closely around him and his father. He became aware that the sounds of shuffling feet and heavy breathing of the Troll warriors were much louder, as if the war band were moving through a fairly confined space.

"I don't think we're in the big cavern anymore," Lithim murmured to Mulng. "I think we've gone into a kind of tunnel."

"I think you're right," Mulng agreed.

A short time later, their surmise was confirmed when they found themselves being guided, by the Trolls on each side of them, into making a sharp turn to the right. Obviously, they had turned a corner in a narrow tunnel.

They tramped on. Lithim suddenly realized that he could very dimly see the shadowy forms of Trolls around him. The torchlight was reflecting off stone walls on each side and a low stone ceiling overhead, providing more illumination than Lithim and Mulng had seen since leaving the Troll community. Lithim suspected that for the Trolls the tunnel was probably as bright as daylight would be for him.

Abruptly, sharply, a Troll voice said, *"Uyurch!"*

On the long journey from Soonchen to here, Lithim had picked up a smattering of Troll words, and he recognized the word he had just heard as meaning "stop" or "halt." He halted at once, wondering what had happened. The Trolls had all stopped instantly, too, as if they were frozen, scarcely even breathing. They seemed to be listening for something.

Lithim became aware of a sound. It was a distant rustling noise, unlike anything he could recall ever hearing, and he tried to liken it to something familiar. A twig being dragged through the dirt might make such a sound, he thought. Or perhaps a crawling snake . . .

His body went cold. He realized that he was hearing the sound of one of the huge underground worms, crawling upon the rock floor. And the sound was drawing nearer.

It was cool and dry in the narrow, rocky tunnel, but Lithim felt perspiration oozing out of his body as the rustling noise grew ever louder. Clearly, the creature making such a sound was enormous. How would the Trolls be able to fight such a thing? he wondered. They appeared to be making no effort to get ready to defend themselves, but remained motionless, controlling their usually noisy breathing so that it could not be heard.

The sound of the monstrous body sliding over rock seemed almost abreast of Lithim now, and still the Trolls did nothing. But the boy became aware that gradually the sound was diminishing—the creature was passing them by! Lithim realized that the great worm must be in an adjoining tunnel, separated by a wall of rock from the one the Trolls and humans were in. He understood why the Trolls had striven for silence: The rock wall would prevent the worm from being able to see or smell anything, but it probably had acutely sharp hearing, and a sound might have brought it smashing through the rock to attack them.

Only when the sound of the worm's crawling had completely faded away did the Trolls resume moving again. The one nearest Lithim grunted something and gave the boy a gentle nudge to make him understand that it was safe to walk once more.

"That was a rather frightening experience, eh?" commented Mulng in a whisper.

"Yes!" Lithim answered, keeping his voice a whisper, too. "I don't think even magic would have been of any use against *that*."

The march quickly settled back into routine. After a time, an increase in the darkness and a lessening of the sounds of shuffling feet and Troll breathing led Lithim to feel that either the tunnel had widened considerably, or else they had left it entirely and were now moving through another large cavern.

To Lithim's amazement, the "noontime" stop was at the edge of what seemed to be a vast underground lake. The boy had not considered that such a thing might be possible. The Trolls unwrapped a large net they had brought with them, woven of strands of leather, and several of them waded into the black water, spreading the net as they went. After a time, they reemerged onto the rocky beach with the net wound around a number of writhing, flopping things that, Lithim discovered when he saw them clearly in the firelight, were eyeless, white-skinned fish. The Trolls quickly gutted them all; spitted them on slim, hard sticks, which had obviously been brought along for just such a purpose; and roasted them in the campfire. Receiving one to eat, Lithim found that it tasted just as delicious as any freshly caught fish from an aboveground lake or river. It was a very welcome change from the dried meat of the last three meals.

New torches were kindled from the campfire, and the journey proceeded. Lithim was relieved to know that it was now just about half over, for he found that the long march through total darkness was wearing away at his nerves; he sometimes felt as if the blackness were going to smother him and had to fight off hysteria. He suspected that his father felt much the same, for Mulng was far less talkative and high-spirited than usual.

At the end of the "day's" travel, supper was once again dried meat with water from the lake, from which the Trolls had filled their water bags. Breakfast, of course, was the same. Midway through the "morning" part of the third day of travel, Lithim became aware that the party had again entered a tunnel of some sort. This tunnel seemed far longer than the other one had been, and Lithim began to speculate on the possibility of encountering another worm. As time wore on, it seemed to him that the surroundings were becoming visible, and eventually he found that he was able to see just about as well as he could at twilight aboveground. This was because the walls and ceiling of the tunnel were covered with some substance that gave off a faint greenish glow.

Abruptly, the procession emerged from the tunnel into a large cavern, which was also lit by a faint glow. As the Trolls and humans tramped along, they passed a cluster of rocks out of which spewed a twisting, swirling spume of gray-white vapor; and moments later, another billowing cloud of vapor, on the opposite side, was passed. Lithim felt a thrill course through his body as he realized they must have reached the cavern of the Undying One. He remembered Gwolchmig saying, "She dwells in a cavern where vapors ooze up out of the very depths of earth," that night at the mage council, when the Troll had first suggested this journey.

The Troll warriors seemed much more relaxed now, and the boy surmised that there was not much danger from worms or other creatures here in the oracle's domain. He took a deep breath, gratified both by the pleasant feeling of safety and the delight of having enough light to be able to see things, even though only at very close range. It was not much different from being in a forest when night was just beginning to close in— far more pleasant than the constant, menacing utter darkness of the last two journey periods. "This is good," he stated, in a normal tone of voice rather than the subdued whisper he had been using.

"Yes, a great relief," said Mulng.

The procession moved steadily on until Gwolchmig called a halt for rest and food beside another faintly hissing vapor vent. Lithim was philosophically munching on still another chunk of dried meat when he noticed that the Trolls around him had suddenly become alerted to something and were all peering in the direction toward which the party had been heading. Looking that way, Lithim saw nothing for a moment. Then several moving shapes became indistinctly visible in the faint, vapor-fogged luminescence.

They moved with almost comical slowness, and with a lurching motion that suggested they might lose balance and fall at any moment. Purposefully, but without any sense of menace, they were heading for the group of seated and reclining Trolls and humans. When they were near enough to be distinctly seen, Lithim gave an involuntary gasp of horrified disgust and heard his father utter a soft exclamation. The Troll warriors around them shifted nervously, staring at the approaching figures with obvious discomfort.

The creatures were Trolls, but they were not like any Trolls Lithim had ever seen. Their skin seemed to be shrunken tightly around their bones, so that instead of the massive legs and arms of a typical Troll, they had thin, insectlike limbs. Their long noses, unlike a fleshy, bulbous Troll nose, were pointed spikes. Their skins were a pallid white, and their eyes were invisible in dark, sunken pits. Lithim suddenly understood that these were servants of the Undying One, Trolls that had been long dead but had been given a kind of false life by a Magic of Darkness. He shivered. This was what Gwolchmig would become.

Gwolchmig had risen to his feet and stood watching the approaching creatures with an expressionless face. They lurched to a stop several paces from him, and one of them opened its mouth. "Why have thou come?" it said in a voice that seemed to echo in its throat. The words were spoken in the ancient language of magic, which Lithim had been taught by his father. The boy understood them, but he saw that the dead Troll's lips did not move when it spoke, and he knew that someone else, far distant, was speaking through its mouth.

"We have come to ask a question," said Gwolchmig in the same language. "We will pay the price."

"Come, then," said the voice from the dead Troll, and the servants of Gurda turned as one and began to shamble back the way they had come.

Gwolchmig glanced back at the Troll warriors and humans. "Let us follow them," he urged.

The group scrambled to its feet, and with Gwolchmig and Kulglitch in the lead, moved after the lurching, indistinct figures. It was necessary to move slowly to keep pace with the dragging footsteps of the living-dead Trolls, and after what seemed an interminable time to Lithim, they came to a place where five fissures in the rocky floor, from which thin streams of vapor were curling upward, formed a rough circle. Standing just outside the circle was a creature that could only be the one known to Trolls as Gurda, the Undying One. Her little group of servants trudged off to one side and joined a crowd of others of their kind, ranged there in a silent, unmoving mass.

Lithim was surprised at the sight of the oracle. He had expected her to be somewhat like a Troll, broad and imposing, but she was small, midway between a human and one of the Little People in size. Her body appeared to be wizened, spindly, and white as the fish in the underground lake, but little could be seen of it, for her long gray-white hair hung about her like a robe. Her eyes were large and gleamed with a faint yellow luminescence. The lower part of her face protruded slightly, like the muzzle of an animal, and made Lithim think of a rat. Unmoving and expressionless, she watched the Trolls and humans come toward her.

At a word from Gwolchmig, the Troll warriors shuffled to a halt some dozen paces from the smoky circle. Lithim and Mulng stopped with them. Drawing a deep breath, Gwolchmig slowly paced forward alone until he stood just an arm's length from the oracle. His immense bulk made her seem even tinier.

"Oh Gurda," he said, speaking slowly and carefully in the tongue of magic, "we have come to ask a question about the event that is known as the Earthdoom."

"I know of it," said Gurda in a voice that creaked with age. "What is thy question?"

The Troll licked his lips with his pointed purple tongue. "Oh Gurda, the Foreseeing that revealed the Earthdoom indicated that the doom might be prevented or altered by the efforts of mages of all the world's thinking races working together. Thus, we know there is a way to fight the unknown Sky Creatures that are bringing the Earthdoom and make them desist from their destruction of our world. But we do not know how the Sky Creatures should be fought. Many ways have been suggested, but all are uncertain. So the question is, oh Gurda, what is it that we must do to prevent the Sky Creatures from destroying the world?"

Lithim held his breath, awaiting the oracle's answer. She turned and shuffled into the circle of smoking vents, halting in the center of it. She remained motionless and silent for a time, with her back to the Trolls and humans, and Lithim had the feeling that she was gathering her strength. Then, slowly, she raised her arms. For the first time, Lithim saw that she held a mage staff. It was not made of wood like those of most mages, but seemed to be a short, smooth rod of some multicolored stone.

Her arms stretched wide, Gurda threw back her head, and a kind of whining moan began to issue from her throat. After a few moments, Lithim became aware that the vapors wafting up from the five fissures in the rock floor were beginning to thicken and pour forth more rapidly. He suddenly felt oddly giddy. The body of the oracle was quickly hidden from sight by the billowing vapors that, instead of continuing to rise, spread outward, hanging in the air and growing ever thicker. Through the growing cloud came Gurda's voice, stronger and deeper than it had been when she was speaking to Gwolchmig, intoning a kind of singsong chant.

Ten thousand great trees and more must thou cut down.
From them strip all leaves, limbs, and bark.
Upon high hills, broad barrens, and in open lands
throughout the world,
let them be raised up again to point at the sky,
a thousand in each place forming a single great design
of circle, square, or three-pointed angle,
exact and perfect in shape,
thousands of paces in length and width.
On the first night of the time of the Earthdoom
let them all be instantly and entirely set afire,
at the same moment, everywhere they stand upon the world.
Then shall those who would despoil the Earth
be halted in their plans.

Her voice faded away and there was silence. Her undead servants stood motionless; the Troll warriors began to shift nervously and mutter to one another.

"Did you follow everything she said, Lith?" Mulng questioned, turning to look at his son.

Lithim nodded. "She wants us to make huge designs, like circles and squares, out of logs, on hilltops and open places. On the night the Sky Creatures arrive, every log in every one of the designs is to be set afire at the same time." He gnawed at his lip. "I understood the words, Father, but I don't understand what this will *do*. It doesn't seem like a weapon. It doesn't even seem like magic."

"No, it does not," Mulng agreed, "but she is a creature we know nothing of, and perhaps her kind of magery is far different from ours. I must ask Gwolchmig if—" His eyes widened. "Gwolchmig!" he exclaimed, whirling to look toward the elderly Troll. Lithim, too, suddenly remembered what had been driven out of his thoughts by this whole episode: Gwolchmig was now doomed to pay the terrible price for the asking of the question. Like his father, Lithim turned stricken eyes toward the Troll.

Gwolchmig stood unmoving, his body almost defiantly erect. Shortly, the little form of the oracle emerged from the thick vapor and paced toward him.

"Thou hast asked thy question and received thine answer," she creaked. "Where, now, is the one who is to become my servant?"

"I am that one," said Gwolchmig firmly.

Gurda took a step backward and stared up at him. "Thou? Thou art a High Wizard!"

"Nevertheless," said Gwolchmig, "I must be the one who pays the price. There is no other."

She continued to stare at him for several moments more, then she said, "Very well."

Lithim felt his father stir beside him. "I cannot let this happen," muttered Mulng, and to Lithim's concern, Mulng strode forward until he stood before the oracle. She did not move, but her golden-hued eyes flicked up to the man's face.

"Great Oracle," said Mulng, speaking in the ancient tongue of magic as Gwolchmig and Gurda had, "I beg thee not to cause this Troll's death."

Lithim's thoughts were shrieking in dismay; she'll kill him, she'll have her dead Troll slaves rip him to pieces, she'll hurl a Bolt of Power at him! With furiously pounding heart, he waited for whatever was to happen as a result of his father's boldness.

What happened was that Gurda simply asked, "Why not?" Lithim blinked and began to feel a touch of relief. She did not seem angry; it was more as if she were just curious.

"Great Oracle," said Mulng, "as thou hast said, he is a High Wizard, and thus, as thou know, he has great knowledge and power. The loss of that knowledge and power would be a dreadful misfortune, to his people and to the whole world, for he has taken a great part in the fight to save the world from the Earthdoom, and that part is not yet over. He is *needed* by the world. Is one more servant for thee more important than the need of the world?"

"No," said Gurda, "it is not." It seemed to Lithim as if she had wanted Mulng to say exactly what he had said.

She turned to Gwolchmig. "Troll, thy people call me Undying One, but a time shall come when I will surely die, for my people were long-lived but not immortal. However, until that time comes, I have an interest in the welfare of the world, and a duty to it. It was needful for thee to come to me, as I think thou know, for as thou have said, it was shown in the Foreseeing that mages of all the world's thinking races must take part in the saving of the world from the Earthdoom, and thus I had a part. Well, my part is done, but as this human has said, thine is not, yet. Thou may still be needed for the work against the Earthdoom, so I will not accept thee as payment. There will be no price, this time, for the answering of a question. Go thou, then. Our business is now finished." She turned and stepped back into the cloud of vapor.

Gwolchmig stared after her, his huge shoulders oddly hunched. Then he looked at Mulng, who threw an arm about his shoulders. Kulglitch shuffled eagerly forward to embrace him. With eyes moist but a grin stretching his mouth, Lithim reached out with mind-touch to give the distant waiting Gra-kwo the information on what had to be done to prevent the Sky Creatures from destroying the world.

7

"**W**hat do you think of it, Lith-im?" questioned Gra-kwo with mind-touch.

"It's—awesome!" said Lithim in like manner, after searching for a word that would fully do justice to what he was seeing.

The Dragon was far from the boy, in his forest dwelling place, but he knew that Lithim; Mulng; and their friend, the yellow-haired sorceress Natl, were standing at the edge of the open plain some distance east of the village of Soonchen, gazing at the immense circle of logs that was being erected there. The circle was only about one-fifth completed, but more than 150 tall tree trunks, trimmed of bark and branches, stood upright in a great semicircle that formed an imposing curved wall. Even though Gra-kwo had kept Lithim informed of the circle's progress each day during the long trip back from the domain of the Trolls, the boy had not really been prepared for the actual sight of the construction. It was not much taller than the walls of Soonchen, but whereas those walls were uneven and meandering, this circle, as could be seen already, would be perfect, with no bulges, indentations, or lopsidedness.

There were mages who studied the making of such perfect shapes, and Gra-kwo had described to Lithim how, once all the mages of Soonchen had heard the words of Gurda and decided to construct a circle, the mages who knew how to do such things had measured it out. First, a stout wooden post had been driven into the ground on the plain, and an incredible thousand-pace-long rope made of strips of leather tied together had been tied around the post. Then a number of people, holding the rope at intervals to keep it stretched as straight and taut as possible, had begun to pace around the post. At every eight paces made by the person holding the end of the rope, farthest out from the post, a large rock was put down as a marker. When the walk around the post was completed, there were 785 rocks, each eight paces apart, forming a perfect circle two thousand paces across. Where each rock had been placed a deep hole, about a pace wide, was dug. Meanwhile, out in the small forest to the north of Soonchen, where Gra-kwo resided, groups of men and women worked to cut down hundreds of trees of the right thickness and trim them of branches and bark. The smooth log poles were then dragged to the plain by teams of people and put into position upright in the holes.

"We started work the day after Gra-kwo gave us

Lithim's message about Gurda's answer," Natl said to Mulng, "and the work has been going on, snowfall or sunshine, every day since—twenty-three days. We're managing to put up seven logs a day, and it has been calculated the circle will be finished about two or three days before the Moon of Budding Trees begins."

"That's not much time before the Sky Creatures are due to arrive," commented Mulng, sounding a trifle worried. "The Trolls were beginning to clear an immense section of forest above their caverns when we left them; they'll use the trees they cut down to construct a huge square within the clearing. They will be finished in time. What about the others?"

"The mages of the Horse People and the mage from the land across the Southern Sea set out to return to their domains at once," said Natl. "They, too, planned to erect circles and pledged they would finish in time. The Little People are working to put great triangles upon flat hilltops in their territories, and I have no doubt but that they will finish in plenty of time—they are like ants in the way they work together to accomplish things."

"Well, with the help of the Mother, everything will be ready when the Sky Creatures come," said Mulng. He tugged thoughtfully at his beard. "Does everyone, everywhere, know what to do when that happens?"

Natl nodded. "Gra-kwo has arranged things. There will be a Dragon at each one of the constructions, and on the evening the Sky Creatures have arrived, as soon as it is fully dark everywhere, Gra-kwo will signal all the other Dragons with mind-touch at the same moment. They will all instantly give the signal to the mages at the constructions, and the mages will immediately set the constructions afire with spells so that they will all blaze up at the same time everywhere, as Gurda indicated."

"Excellent!" Mulng jerked his head in a sharp nod of satisfaction. "All is indeed ready, then."

Natl sighed and eyed him with her head cocked to one side. "I must tell you, Mulng, that I and others are not so sure of all this. As far as I can see, these big constructions are just going to turn into fiery designs. I can't see any magic in them, and I can't see how they could do anything to the Sky Creatures that would make them stop whatever they might be doing. There was some bitter argument in the council before we all finally agreed to do what the Undying One said. Some insisted that it was all nonsense and that we should ignore it and devise some way of fighting the Sky Creatures with magic we understand, as we were originally trying to do before Gwolchmig told us of this oracle of his." She grimaced. "I hope we are not making a terrible mistake by pinning our faith on these wooden designs!"

"It is no mistake," Mulng said firmly. "Remember the words of Alglinnadorn—without the help of Gurda, the last mage of a thinking race, the promise of the Foreseeing could not be fulfilled. Gurda spoke of this, too. These things she has told us to build will be the world's salvation!"

Despite Mulng's words, Natl continued to look doubtful, and Lithim eyed her thoughtfully. He found himself in agreement with her. He, too, could not understand how the huge wooden constructions Gurda had told them to build could actually do anything to make the

Sky Creatures halt their planned destruction of the world. If there was any magic in them, it was magic of a kind he did not know. It made him feel a bit guilty to be in disagreement with his father, but nevertheless he was. He hoped he was wrong.

"Do you think these wooden designs are going to work the way we hope?" he asked Gra-kwo.

"This one does not understand/comprehend/foresee how they will function, Lith-im. This one thinks we must have faith in the oracle's prediction, as the Trolls do."

Lithim sighed. No one seemed to have the slightest idea what all the huge wooden shapes would do.

Notwithstanding his doubts, Lithim did his part, in the following days, to help get the circle of logs finished in time, as did Natl and Mulng. The work was arranged and organized by Soonchen's village Chieftain, Leng, who was, of course, skilled in such things. Some days Lithim found himself appointed to work on the plain, helping to raise logs into position in the holes. This was done by pushing a log to the edge of a hole, then hauling it upright with leathern ropes until it slid into place. At other times Lithim was assigned to labor with groups of people who dragged logs from the forest to the circle's site. All this work went on, as Natl had said, whether the sun was brightly shining or whether snow was pouring down out of an ash gray sky. Actually, snow made the task of dragging logs much easier; they slid more smoothly and quickly upon snow-covered ground.

Just about everyone in Soonchen was involved in the work, including small children, who could do little more than peel bark off a tree trunk, and elderly people, who had just enough strength to hack off tree limbs with stone hand axes. It all helped. Gra-kwo, too, did his part, proving immensely useful in being able to drag several logs at a time from the forest to the plain. Even the Chieftain and his counselors shared in the hard labor. The only ones who refused to help in any way were the four priestesses of the Soonchen Temple of the Mother, for they, like all the priestesses of the Atlan religion, refused to acknowledge that the Earthdoom would occur. They regarded it as blasphemy to believe that the world—the Mother herself—could be damaged or destroyed. They had been ordered by the Chieftain not to interfere with what was being done to try to prevent the Earthdoom; and so they simply sulked within the temple, ignoring the feverish bustle in the village and calling down curses upon the mages, who, in their opinion, were misleading the villagers into sacrilege.

The Moon of Long Nights came to an end, giving way to the Moon of Coldest Days, which left only three full moons until the coming of the Sky Creatures. As if to be in accord with the moon's name, the weather turned bitterly cold, but still the work of erecting the great woodhenge went on. Similar work continued everywhere else, as well: the Little People toiling to put a pair of vast triangles on adjoining hilltops, the Trolls stolidly building a mammoth square in the great clearing they had made, the dark-skinned people of Molo raising a giant circle in the northern desert region of their land, the Horse People of the East making still another circle on a great brown plain that was a sea of grass in summertime.

There were accidents, setbacks, and delays. In the forest near Soonchen, several of the woodcutters were killed when a tree trunk twisted as it fell and smashed into them. In the Molo desert, an early sandstorm piled up tons of sand against the log circle, nearly burying a portion of it. It took many days to clear the sand away. In the territory of the Little People, work was slowed down by frequent blizzards. But nowhere did the work slacken for more than the time it took to deal with the setback. Time lost was made up by extra effort, with workers sometimes toiling well into the night, by torchlight. Most everyone involved in the building of the great wooden circles, squares, and triangles felt that only the completion of their work in time could save the world from the doom that was rushing toward it. Even those, like Lithim and Natl, who were not sure of the usefulness of the constructions shared in the toil in the hope that they were wrong and that the words of Gurda— "Then shall those who would despoil the Earth be halted in their plans"—would be borne out.

Rumors of all these awesome constructions that were being built eventually drifted to Atlan Isle and reached the ears of the Atlan High Chieftain, Tlon. He clenched his teeth and scowled when he heard of the great circle being erected by the villagers and mages of Soonchen. Only a few moons previously, he had led a large war band to Soonchen, intent upon massacring the mages and punishing the villagers for disobeying his order to ignore the blasphemous teaching known as the Earthdoom. But his war band had been routed by a magical attack—despite the help of a mysterious wizard who had attached himself to the war band—and had barely managed to get back to Atlan Isle with less than half its original numbers. Tlon's hatred of the mages gathered in Soonchen was like a sharp-toothed animal crouched inside his stomach and trying to gnaw its way out. He prayed to the Mother that their ring of upright logs might topple over and crush them all!

However, the more Tlon thought about the huge woodhenge being built at Soonchen, the more he wondered why the mages were building it. The rumors implied that it was to be a magical weapon to prevent the Earthdoom, but Tlon had been assured by Chuln, the High Priestess of the Daughters of the Mother, that the Earthdoom was nothing but a fake, a doctrine created by the mages to frighten ordinary people and gain power over them. Tlon was young, inexperienced, and not very bright; but nevertheless, it seemed odd to him that the mages would spend so much time and effort constructing a weapon against something they knew would not happen. It occurred to him for the first time that perhaps the mages really believed in the Earthdoom and were legitimately trying to do something to prevent it. He began to worry about this and finally confronted the High Priestess about it.

Chuln gave him a scathing look. "The mages are simply having the thing built in order to convince people of their power. When the end of the year comes and this Earthdoom they have been predicting does not happen, they will tell everyone that it was their circle of logs that prevented it!''

Hesitantly Tlon said, ''But it is rumored that the Little People and the Trolls are building such things, too. Why would they—''

''It is rumored, it is rumored,'' mocked Chuln, interrupting him. ''Those rumors were started by the mages, Chieftain. They know that no one can get into the territories of the Little People or the domain of the Trolls to learn the truth, so they made up these rumors to frighten those foolish enough to believe them.'' That she regarded Tlon as one of those foolish people was obvious, but although he resented her openly contemptuous behavior toward him, he did feel sufficiently foolish at having been momentarily fearful, so he swallowed his resentment and quickly departed from her.

The Moon of Coldest Days came to an end, and Storm Moon began. Fortunately for those working on the constructions, it produced a series of very cold but calm days, and the work progressed well. By the moon's end, the Trolls had finished their huge square in the cleared area above their underground caverns, and the triangles in the territories of the Little People had been completed as well. The Soonchen Circle, as it was called by those building it, was more than three-fourths done.

The Moon of Rains began, and thus there was only one whole moon and a few days before the coming of the Sky Creatures. At Soonchen, in the Molo Desert, and on the plain of the Horse People, humans began to glance fearfully at the sky as they worked to complete their wooden circles. Each sundown, as the Trolls came issuing forth from their caverns like ants from an anthill to hunt and forage in the forest, they raised their pale eyes to study the sky—visible now, above the area they had cleared—for a sign of the alien creatures from beyond the stars. On their mountaintops, Dragon mages began to keep watch.

A night of full darkness bespoke the end of the Moon of Rains, and with sunrise dawned the Moon of Budding Trees, the last moon of the year, during which the year would end and a new year begin. Some time within the next few days, the world would face the Earthdoom.

Even as the first day of the Moon of Budding Trees dawned, the five vessels of The Industrious Ones were passing through the farthermost portion of the orbit of Mars, some 248 million miles from Earth. On the vessels' vision instruments the surface of Earth now showed as clearly as if each craft were hovering no more than a hundred miles or so above it. The sinuous, gleaming curls of rivers could be seen; mountain ranges appeared as long stretches of corrugated texture; forests were huge patches of mottled green. Aboard each vessel, at the same precise moment, a communications device made a report.

"—MEAN-DISTANCE-OF-SELECTED-OBJECT-POINT-NINE-THREE-TWO-LIGHTSPEED-SEG-MENTS—."

The report was received within the mind of each of the creatures aboard each vessel, who communicated with one another and with their vessel itself by means of instantaneous electronic thought transference. In this same manner, The Industrious One who had been designated as Director, or leader of the five vessels and their crews, now issued an order.

"—commence braking procedures—."

Aboard each vessel, the machinery responsible for controlling speed and direction was motivated by the Director's order to begin performing certain functions, and imperceptibly, the vessels began to lose speed. By the time they reached Earth, they would be able to enter its atmosphere at a speed slow enough to prevent the friction of their passage from burning the air through which they moved, as the flight of a meteor would do.

Normally, a communication by one of The Industrious Ones was sent to and received by all the others on the five ships, but by more or less "switching bands" within its mind, one of the creatures could communicate with another without being "heard" by the rest. On the Director's vessel, The Industrious One whose designation was the Representative of the Path now communicated in this fashion with the Director.

"—it must be reminded that upon arrival above the planetary surface there must be one last scan made to detect intelligence—."

"—a reminder is not necessary—the scan will be made—," the Director responded. Then it added, "—although it will be a waste of energy and time—."

The two creatures regarded each other. Had another Industrious One been watching them, familiar with the body movements and "facial" expressions of its kind, it would have instantly recognized that the Director and the Representative of the Path bore a deep dislike for each other.

8

Lithim was dreaming, and it was a pleasant dream, but someone was trying to interrupt it. *"Lith-im, awaken,"* a voice was saying over and over, and finally the dream evaporated and the boy's mind swam up into consciousness. He opened his eyes upon the darkness of the cubicle in the Soonchen guesthouse where he lay next to his father. Mulng was sound asleep, breathing regularly with a faint snore, and no one else was in the cubicle or at its entrance, so who had spoken?

"Lith-im, are you awake?" The boy realized it had been Gra-kwo's mind-touch that had awakened him.

"Oh, Gra-kwo. Yes. What is it? What's the matter?"

"This one knows you were asleep, Lith-im, but something important is happening. This one thought you would want to know about it. Look at the sky, Lith-im."

The sky. Lithim could think of only one reason why Gra-kwo so urgently wanted him to look at the sky. His heart beginning to pound, he rose from his pile of furs, clutched his cloak about himself, and tiptoed down the narrow corridor outside the cubicle until he came to the guesthouse entrance. A curtain of furred animal skins closed it off, and, pushing past this, Lithim stepped outside into the chill night and looked upward into the star-filled sky. He scanned it slowly for a few moments; then his breath caught in his throat as he saw what Grakwo wanted him to see. In the east there was a strange new constellation in the sky. Five points of light, arranged in a perfectly straight row, hung glittering where none had been before.

"It's them, isn't it?" said Lithim with mind-touch. "The Sky Creatures. They've come."

"It seems so, Lith-im. This one has contacted his master, Klo-gra-hwurg-ka-urgu-nga, and he confirms it. They are not quite here yet, but they are swiftly approaching."

"But they aren't moving," Lithim objected. "They're just hanging there."

"They do not seem to be moving, but they are," Grakwo told him. *"The watchers of the Beautiful People have been observing/viewing/scrutinizing them since early darkness, and they have slowly dropped lower in reference to a certain mountain peak. My master thinks they are still so far away that their movement is not discernible/detectable/noticeable."*

"Are their vessels stars, then?" wondered Lithim, amazed, for the shining lights looked just like the stars around them. Most people of Atlan believed stars were lights that had been created by the Mother to help light the sky at night, and Lithim could not understand how these alien beings could be using them as conveyances.

"Our watchers think they are movable dwellings of some sort"—Gra-kwo's mind-touch conveyed a faint suggestion of moving oval shapes—*"but what causes them to glow like stars we do not know."*

Lithim heard a rustle of movement behind him and glanced around. A figure, cloak clutched around itself as his was, had just emerged from the guesthouse. He saw that it was Natl.

"I was awake and I heard you go past my sleeping niche, Lithim," she told him in a whisper. "I felt that something might be wrong. Is it?"

"Look at the sky," he urged her. "A little to the left of the roof of the Chieftain's dwelling."

After a moment, he heard her gasp as he had done. "That row of stars—it's *them,* isn't it, Lith?"

"Yes. Gra-kwo says some of the Dragons have been watching them since early night. It doesn't look as if they are moving, but they are." He switched to mind-touch. "Gra-kwo, do your watchers have any idea when the Sky Creatures will actually get here?"

"One of the watchers is one who has learned to do much with numbers and measurements," replied the Dragon. *"Based upon the amount of time it has taken the Sky Things to move in reference to the mountain peak, he thinks they will be here by midday."*

Midday. Lithim felt a shock, as if icy water was suddenly flowing through his body. Eight moons ago, the arrival of the Sky Creatures had seemed to be far in the future; and even a moon ago, it had been possible for him to think of their coming as a distant event. Now, when the sun rose in the morning, it would be the Day of the Earthdoom!

"Gra-kwo says they will be here by midday," he told Natl.

"May the Mother be with us," he heard her whisper in prayer.

"Mother be with us," he murmured in echo. Saying a prayer to the Mother made him think of the Daughters of the Mother, the priestesses, who had insisted that the Sky Creatures did not exist and that the Earthdoom was a hoax. They had tried to have him, his father, and Natl executed for blasphemy, and when they were thwarted in that, they had tried to murder his father. "We ought to go to the temple and wake up the Daughters and make them look at this," he said, a malicious note in his voice. "I wonder what they would have to say now?"

"I don't think even this would make them believe, Lith," replied Natl thoughtfully. "I think that right up to the moment the Earthdoom begins, if we can't prevent it, they'll find some way of convincing themselves that it isn't really going to happen."

"I can't understand them!" the boy said vehemently. "I still believe in the Mother; none of this has changed that. This doesn't mean that She isn't really there; it just means that some of the things *we* thought about her were wrong. Why can't they accept that? How could they close their eyes to the truth of the Foreseeing, and how can they close their eyes to the truth of *this?*" He gestured toward the row of lights.

"I don't think they can dare admit to themselves that

they were wrong about the coming of the Sky Creatures," Natl told him, "because that could show them that they might have been wrong about a lot of other things. They couldn't stand that. It would destroy them."

Lithim sighed. "Well, whether they believe or not doesn't matter. The Sky Creatures are here, and I hope we're ready for them. I think I ought to wake up my father—he'll want to know what's happening." And within a short time Mulng, too, was standing with his eyes raised to the sky.

Throughout the parts of the world where the five thinking races dwelt, many others were also aware of the coming of the Sky Creatures. From their mountain heights, the Dragons had been watching the oncoming vessels since a few hours after sunset; and the Trolls, out doing their nightly hunting and foraging, had soon become aware of them. As night drew toward dawn, many humans who rose early to begin their day's hunting, fishing, or other tasks soon noticed the string of lights.

Like the star known as the Star of Dawn, which often stayed brightly shining until well into morning, the five lights were still visible after sunrise and were eventually seen by just about everyone in the Atlan Domain, the territories of the Little People, and the faraway lands of Molo and of the Horse People. In Atlan villages where the Daughters of the Mother had managed to suppress all knowledge of the Earthdoom, there was wonder and speculation and a kind of amused excitement, but where the coming of the Sky Creatures had been expected, the faces of those looking upward were grim and filled with dread.

The mages of Soonchen and all the villagers, from the Chieftain down to the lowliest, left the village and made their way to the great circle of logs on the plain. On this day, all work, hunting, fishing, and food gathering was suspended. Throughout their territories, the tribes of the Little People began to converge upon the hills where they had erected their triangles. In their caverns beneath the Great Forest, most Trolls stolidly prepared for sleep. A few wakeful ones, such as Gwolchmig and Kulglitch, awaited the coming of night. From the mountaintops, Dragons soared up and fanned out, each proceeding to a place where one of the wooden constructions stood.

As the morning grew brighter, the lights in the sky faded from sight, their glow finally obscured by sunlight. Lithim, his father, and Natl sat with the rest of the Sooncheners in a great crowd gathered around the log circle. Only the four Daughters of the Mother had remained within the village, in their temple. They, too, had seen the row of glowing lights, but, as Natl had predicted, they did not accept them as the vessels of the Sky Creatures. After some discussion, the priestesses had decided to believe them to be a sign from the Mother—a warning against belief in the Earthdoom.

The morning wore on. Gra-kwo came gliding down out of the sky to land with a thump near the crowd of humans. Only a few moons earlier, the Soonchen villagers would have been terrified by the nearness of the great green-scaled Dragon. Now they virtually accepted him as one of themselves, as they did the slim, pale-eyed, silvery-haired Alfar woman, Alglinnadorn. Dragons, Alfar, Little People, and even the Trolls were now joined with humanity, in the minds of most humans, as fellow earth-creatures. They were all united against the common menace that sought to destroy them and their world.

Lithim sent a thought to his Dragon friend. "It is hard to have to just sit and wait, isn't it, Gra-kwo?"

"Perhaps it is easier for one of the Beautiful People to do that than for one of your kind," replied the Dragon pensively. *"Perhaps we have more patience because we live so much longer than you do. But neither of us can do anything but wait, Lith-im, until nightfall."*

Yes, we can only wait until nightfall, thought Lithim. But I hope the world isn't destroyed before then—before we have a chance to strike at the Sky Things. He stared at the curving wall of tall logs stretching before him. Peeled of all bark, they looked almost white in the sunlight. What can they do? he wondered, as he had many times before. Is there some unknown ancient magic that is going to leap out of the circle when we set it afire? Gurda prophesied that if we built such things as this, they would prevent the Earthdoom, and the Trolls believe in her prophesy without any doubt. But I hope to the Mother they're right! He sighed.

The waiting went on. Eventually, the sun stood straight overhead, and Lithim anxiously scanned the sky, knowing the Dragons felt sure that noontime was when the Sky Creatures would appear over the world. He saw nothing, and nothing seemed to be happening.

80

Imperceptibly, the sun began its downward movement in the west. The boy relaxed.

Then, suddenly, although the day was bright and cloudless, there was a sound like a long, rippling rumble of thunder in the distance. The vessels of The Industrious Ones had entered Earth's atmosphere at slightly more than the speed of sound, and the sonic boom created by their entrance reverberated through the air.

Heads jerked upward, and the crowd of Sooncheners fell totally silent. Their faces strained with fear of the unknown, the mages and villagers peered into the sky, wondering how there could be thunder on a sunny, cloudless day. That it had something to do with the Sky Creatures they had no doubt.

"Look there!" shrieked a villager, leaping to her feet and pointing. An object had appeared, hanging dark and tiny, far distant in the western sky.

The vessels of The Industrious Ones had spread out in a semicircle over Earth's northern hemisphere and taken up position at a height of some ten thousand feet while their instruments conducted a systematic scan for signs of intelligent life on the planet below, as the Representative of the Path had demanded. However, the instruments were searching for signs of intelligence only as The Industrious Ones conceived it, and so all their reports were coming in negative. "—NO-INDICATION-OF-ELECTRONIC-ACTIVITY—NO-INDICATION-OF-NUCLEAR-FUSION-ACTIVITY—NO-INDICATION-OF-ARTIFICIAL-MAGNETIC-GRAVITATIONAL-ACTIVITY—NO-EMISSION-FROM-COMMUNICATIONS-DEVICES—."

"—*cease scanning*—," ordered the Director from his ship, which by chance was hanging directly over Atlan Isle. "—*no sign of intelligent life is apparent—commence oceanic and continental metallic ore liberation operations*—."

The Industrious Ones began their mission.

9

High Chieftain Tlon, son of Mleng Bearslayer, had arisen early to prepare for a boar hunt in the woods to the north of the city of Atlan Dis on Atlan Isle. After donning his clothing, he had stepped outside his dwelling to check the weather. Almost at once, he saw the five stars that had never been there before. For moments he stared in amazement. "Do you see that row of stars?" he demanded of the warrior who was standing guard at the dwelling's entrance.

The man cleared his throat nervously. "Yes, High Chieftain. They've been there since I came on duty. The guard who was here before me said they were there when he came on duty, too."

"They were never there before," protested Tlon, continuing to stare with fascination. "Where in the Mother's name did they come from?"

"I don't know, High Chieftain."

Tlon pondered. He had never heard of such a thing as this ever happening before; not even the oldest legends mentioned such an event. The sudden appearance in the sky of five new stars, arranged in an even, eye-catching row, must be an omen of major significance. His first thought was that the Mother must have placed them there. But why? What did they mean?

"Go to the temple and ask the Daughters about this," he ordered the guardsman. "Find out if they know what it means and come back and report to me."

The man hurried off. The priestess who slid the temple portal aside in answer to his thumpings on it was at first cross and belligerent at having been awakened so early; but when, at the man's urgings, she stepped out and saw the five mysterious lights, her manner changed. She hurried to awaken her superior, and shortly, every priestess associated with the temple, including High Priestess Chuln, was awake and outside gazing at the sky.

"What shall I tell the High Chieftain?" persisted the guardsman.

"Tell him that this is surely a sign from the Mother," snapped Chuln. "She has probably done it as a warning to those heretical mages and their followers in Soonchen." But as the man trotted off to report, she turned to one of the lesser priestesses. "Consult the Book of the Mother," she ordered. "See if anything like this is spoken of." She glanced up at the sky with a faint frown of worry creasing her forehead.

Tlon and a group of his cronies went on their hunt. They emerged from the forest shortly after noon, two men carrying the body of a boar slung from a pole. With boasts and jests flying loudly among them, the men tramped down the narrow trail that led back to Atlan Dis. After a time, one of the men chanced to glance at the sky.

"Great Mother!" he shouted, stopping in his tracks. "What is that?"

Tlon looked up and froze. He beheld the Director of The Industrious Ones' vessel, poised in the sky above the island. It had dropped lower than the rest of the vessels and was clearly visible as a dark triangular shape. The ships of The Industrious Ones were more than a mile in length, in order to be able to carry large amounts of cargo, and Tlon could judge the hugeness of the thing he was observing. It seemed to him like an ominous weapon, a gigantic spearpoint, threatening him. He stared up at it in horror. First the row of new stars and now this; it was obvious that something strange was going on in the sky, and Tlon did not think that the Mother had anything to do with it. He was recalling the predictions of the mages about the coming of the Sky Creatures.

"They were right," he declared hoarsely. "The mages were right!" He broke into a run, and his followers quickly pelted after him. The two men carrying the pole with the heavy body of the boar slung from it stumbled and cursed as they tried unsuccessfully to keep up.

Tlon was panting heavily from the long run as he entered the city. He was instantly struck by the silence; usually the maze of streets bustled with people at this time of day, but now it seemed almost deserted. Most of the citizens were huddled inside their dwellings, cowering in fear of the strange apparition overhead. As Tlon, with his men strung out behind him, trotted toward the Temple of the Mother, he passed no more than a handful of people in the streets, all of them standing in silence and staring up at the sky with frightened faces.

Reaching the temple, the High Chieftain stormed into it and glared about. A young priestess was seated cross-legged on the floor near the entrance, meditating. "Where is the Elder Daughter Chuln?" he bawled at her.

Sensing his fury, she scrambled to her feet and fled toward the rear of the building, ducking through curtains that closed off an area of the temple. Tlon squatted down on his toes to catch his breath. He still had his stout boar spear in his hand.

Chuln came striding out past the curtains, the young priestess and several others cowering behind her. She stalked toward Tlon and halted no more than an arm's length from him. He rose to face her.

"How dare you come shouting into this holy place?" she hissed at him. "High Chieftain or not—"

He interrupted her. "Have you seen what is in the sky *now,* Elder Daughter?" he bellowed.

She appeared startled, both at his daring to interrupt her in such a tone and at his question. "What do you mean?" she asked guardedly. She and the other priestesses had not been out of the temple since early morning and were unaware of the object hanging over the island.

"There is a thing in the sky above Atlan Isle, Elder Daughter," Tlon told her through clenched teeth. "A thing you assured me would never be there! The creatures from beyond the stars, which you said did not exist, are *here,* Chuln. They have come. You were wrong and the mages were right. I would that I had listened to them instead of to you!"

"There are no creatures from beyond the stars," she declared angrily, her voice rising. "The Mother never made any creatures but those of *this* world. There are no others!"

It was at this moment that the Director of The Industrious Ones gave the order to begin the work for which the aliens had come to Earth. An invisible beam of energy stabbed down out of the vessel above Atlan Isle and reached into the sea that lapped the island's shores. It probed down through the water; penetrated the rock that was the sea bottom; and entered the mantle, the seething mass of molten rock that lies beneath the world's hard crust. The beam moved in a slow, even semicircle, leaving a wide, curved rent in the ocean floor, through which the red-hot, thick liquid rock of the mantle swiftly welled up into the water. A section of the sea just off the shore of Atlan Isle suddenly exploded into a tumult of steam, with a sound like the roar of an angry giant.

The sound of the explosion followed instantly upon Chuln's words, and her body jerked in surprise, as did Tlon's. Tlon's men had remained in the street outside the temple, but one now thrust his head through the entrance. "High Chieftain," he yelled, obviously near panic, "there is a great cloud of steam pouring up out of the sea!" Tlon and Chuln turned their heads to look at him, the mouths of both identically hanging open.

Like many oceanic islands, Atlan Isle had been built up many thousands of years previously by the eruption of an underwater volcano. Boiling hot lava had poured up from a vent in the ocean floor, just as was happening now. It had gradually formed a cone, the top of which had finally protruded above the water, producing the island. The volcano had been dormant for centuries, but now the slicing energy beam of The Industrious Ones had opened a new vent, through which molten rock began trying to force its way up to the surface. As the pressure mounted, Atlan Isle began to shudder.

Their faces twisted in dismay, Tlon, his henchman, and the priestesses staggered to stay on their feet as the dirt floor of the temple gave a sudden heave. "The mages were right," Tlon yelled in desperation. "This is the Earthdoom! The world is going to be destroyed!"

"No!" Chuln shrieked. "The Mother cannot be harmed. That is heresy!" She reached out a hand toward him, the fingers clawed as if she wanted to tear his flesh. A wave of rage against this woman who, he felt, had betrayed him, swept through Tlon. He drew back his arm and, with a savage thrust, drove the boar spear into the Elder Daughter Chuln's abdomen with such force that its stone point protruded from her back. Chuln made a gargling sound in her throat and sank to her knees, clutching the shaft of the spear with both hands. The other priestesses emitted shrieks of horror.

Tlon turned and stumbled his way to the entrance,

the warrior at his heels. Outside it was as if twilight had suddenly fallen, for a dark, dense cloud of smoke was boiling up out of the hill that marked the island's highest point and was swiftly spreading in all directions. A rain of fine, hot gray ash drifted down out of it like a mist. A faint, steady rumbling noise was coming from the ground. Accompanying it, like a soprano chorus over a bass one, was the sirenlike wail of the voices of the women, children, and men of Atlan Dis, howling in fear, pouring forth from their dwellings and staggering through the city's streets, seeking escape from the terror that had suddenly engulfed them.

"What can we do?" one of Tlon's men yelled.

Tlon suddenly remembered that he was their High Chieftain and they were automatically turning to him for help. He had an inspiration, born of his own mounting fear. "Make for the docks," he shouted. "We will get on a boat. Maybe we'll be safe out on the open water."

He tried to run, but the shivering of the ground permitted no more than a kind of lurching jog. Many of the buildings of Atlan Dis were formed of stones that had simply been piled atop one another, and the ripples of motion in the earth were causing some structures to come apart. Tlon and his men had to scramble over piles of rock that blocked many of the winding ways through the city.

The ways were also thronged with people. Like Tlon, most of them had seized on the hope that they might be safe if only they could get off the shuddering, darkening island; and they, too, were trying to make their way to the docks at the city's edge. They pushed and jostled one another in their panic, literally fighting one another to get through. Tlon quickly found that his rank meant nothing in the face of the hysteria that gripped his people; at one corner a bigger, heavier man blindly thrust him aside so that he fell and gashed a knee. Cursing and almost sobbing, he struggled to his feet and staggered on. He had lost all his retainers by now. They had either been separated from him by the crowds or had gone different ways.

It was becoming difficult to breathe. The ash drifting down out of the dark cloud that now hung over the entire island was as thick as a fog, but, unlike fog, it was formed of particles of solid matter that caught in the throats and lungs of people breathing heavily from exertion. Tlon found himself gasping and choking. The thought flashed quickly through his mind that he had never really appreciated the sweetness of clean, uncontaminated air; he had always just taken it for granted—until now.

Finally reaching the dock area, he was appalled to find himself on the outskirts of a huge, surging, shrieking crowd. Most of the people of Atlan Dis were here, fighting to make their way onto one of the six long stone platforms jutting out into the water, where fishing boats and merchant vessels were tied up. With a sinking heart, Tlon realized that there couldn't possibly be enough boats for all these people. Long before he would be able to get onto one of the quays, the boats would all be gone.

"Let me through!" he howled, trying to push into the crowd. "I am the High Chieftain!" But his voice was lost in the din of other yelling, wailing, cursing voices; and none of these panicked people would have heeded him anyway. He began to beat with his fists at those in front of him, but a sudden surge in the ground sent him staggering back, and, losing his balance, he fell painfully onto his side. The din of the crowd swelled in volume with the tremor.

Tlon rolled over and pulled himself to his hands and knees. Idly, he noticed that the rain of ash was coming down thicker and faster. He could scarcely breathe, and his eyes were stinging painfully. He became aware that the rumbling sound of the earth was growing louder, drowning out the noise of the crowd. The ground was shuddering so violently that most of the people had been flung down as he had been.

The pressure of thousands of tons of molten rock pushing up out of the earth became too much for the relatively thin wall of stone holding it back. With a titanic roar like a thousand thunderclaps merged into one, the top of the long-dormant volcano that was Atlan Isle blew apart, with pebble-sized, chunk-sized, boulder-sized fragments hurtling thousands of feet in all directions. Half the island had literally vanished at once, and with gouts of glowing red liquid lava now forcing their way up through numerous cracks and crevices, the half that was left began to break apart as well. The water of the sea surged in to fill the spaces that had once been filled by rock; and as cold water met red-hot lava, there was a series of explosions that completed the destruction.

Out on the sea, in water that was as active and surging as if it were at the center of a great storm, the five-man crew of a merchant vessel that had set sail from Atlan Dis only minutes before The Industrious Ones had begun their work stared in horror at the drama of destruction. Where Atlan Isle had sat as a long, dark strip upon the water, there was now a single great cloud of boiling white steam mixed with dark, billowing ash. Chunks of rock from the first explosion that had wracked the island were still raining down around the tiny ship, striking the water with a sound like a handclap and sending explosive splashes high into the air. In days to come, each of these silent, staring men would tell others how they had seen Atlan Isle and the great city of Atlan Dis, home of nearly two thousand humans, sink into the sea.

At the moment when the Director of The Industrious Ones gave the order to begin the work for which the aliens had come, the vessel hanging in the western sky beyond Soonchen left its position and sped off toward the east. "It's gone," cried some of the people who had been watching it in the crowd gathered around the great circle of logs.

Lithim was one of those who had been staring at the speck in the sky. He was able to follow its incredibly swift movement for a moment or two; then it simply seemed to vanish. The abrupt departure of the vessel worried him, for he felt that it had gone somewhere to do something, and he had a sense of dread about what it might do.

The Industrious Ones' craft had gone to the Great Forest. Its instruments had indicated rich amounts of various minerals, particularly two rare metals, in the rock formations beneath a portion of the forest. The craft took up a position above this area and began its mining operations.

On the underside of the ship, at the center of the cargo space, the plastic–metal skin of the hull dilated, producing a wide, circular opening. Out of this, an invisible cone-shaped beam of force reached down to the forest. As if sucked up by a giant vacuum cleaner, trees, soil, and rock went hurtling up to the ship, inside the beam. As this material flowed into the cargo area, it was immediately processed by a number of automatic devices. Organic substances—wood, leaves, soil, and animal life—were volatilized into atoms, which were released into the air around the ship. From the rocky material remaining, the rare metals and other minerals desired by The Industrious Ones were separated out as hot gases. These were sucked into a cooling chamber, where their molecules were quickly slowed down until the gas became molten liquid, which then cooled into dry, hard crystals. Leftover rock and unwanted minerals were reduced to powder, which was allowed to fall back to earth as a dry, dark rain.

The vacuum beam moved swiftly back and forth over the selected area of forest, which was many miles in size. Within minutes, all organic matter covering the rock had been stripped away, and the ancient rock that had once been a chain of hills lay exposed, an enormous, unsightly, barren blotch in the midst of the thick greenery around it. The beam continued to eat into this, stripping away layer after layer of rock, which was pulled up to the vessel, processed, and then returned to the forest as a rain of powdery sand. This rock dust built up on the leaves and limbs and in the crotches of trees, causing branches to eventually sag from the weight until most of the powder slid off and cascaded to the ground below, or else the branch tore loose from the trunk to either fall or hang dangling by strands of wood. Thus, the area of forest around the barren patch began to look like a burned-out place. The ground was completely covered with an ever-increasing layer of ashlike gray powder, out of which broken-limbed trees stuck up like fingers pointing accusingly at the sky.

As the sun slowly and patiently dropped ever lower in the sky, the mining beam of The Industrious Ones continued to suck up rock. The stretch of ancient, worn-down, rocky hills grew ever thinner, while the blighted, powder-covered area around it grew ever wider. There was a steady movement of forest creatures away from this area, but one, who lay soundly sleeping, was unaware of the powdery rain until her form was so covered by it that she was awakened by a sensation of a heavy weight pressing her into the earth.

The Dragon known to her people as Ko-ah-nag had come here to the domain of the Trolls in order to give the Trolls Gra-kwo's signal to set their huge wooden square afire when the time came. She had been asleep since before dawn and was unaware that the Sky Creatures had arrived. Now she opened an eye and sneezed violently; something was tickling her nose. For a moment she thought she was dreaming; then she realized that there really *was* an unseen heavy weight pressing her down. Opening the other eye, she struggled to her feet, noting with astonishment that the ground, which had been the typical leaf-litter of a forest when she had gone to sleep on it, seemed to have become an expanse of soft sand; and sand was sliding off her body as she stood up and shook herself. She also became aware that a steady rain of fine sand was falling all around her, and she sneezed again; some of it had gotten into her nostrils. Staring about in puzzlement at all these odd changes, she saw the beam that was inexorably pulling up mile after mile of rock to The Industrious Ones' vessel. To her, it appeared as a swirling grayish brown cone, hundreds of paces wide at the base and tapering up to a point where it emerged from the vessel that, with her marvelous Dragon eyesight, she could clearly make out. She could not understand what the beam was or what it was doing, for the whole concept of such a thing was beyond her imagination; but she did realize that the Sky Creatures had come and that they were doing something to the forest. Her first thought was that they were destroying all the trees, for she was shocked by the sight of the enormous area of bare rock that had once been covered with trees and soil; but then she saw that the swirling beam was moving back and forth over the rock and ignoring the trees all around it. Ko-ah-nag began to understand that the beam was doing something to the rock, but what?

Taking flight with some difficulty because of the impediment of the rain of sand, she flapped out over the expanse of rock and began to fly around the beam, taking care not to get close to it. Eventually her sharp eyes detected that there seemed to be a slight change in each section of rock the beam passed over. She focused her sight upon a particular rocky bump and saw that it was unmistakably flatter after the beam covered it for a moment. With a flash of understanding, she realized that the rock was being worn away and that the strange swirling cone must actually be composed of worn-away fragments of rock being pulled upward to the vessel of the Sky Creatures. Why they would want to do such as this, unless simply out of malice, she could not imagine, but she could see that if the swirling cone continued to move back and forth over the rock, the rock would eventually all be gone. This meant that the caverns that lay beneath it would then be open and exposed to the sunlight. And in those caverns lived the Trolls, for whom the touch of sunlight was death.

Ko-ah-nag knew she had to do something, and the only thing she could think of was to attack the Sky Creature vessel and try to drive it off before it could finish its work of destruction. Beating her wings, she rose toward it. As she drew closer, she became more aware of its monstrous size, and misgivings filled her; she was dwarfed by the mile-long craft like a fish swimming beside a floating log. She was also bewildered by it, for she had never seen anything like the shiny smoothness of the metal and plastic alloy that formed its hull; and she could well have believed it was a huge living creature, except that her senses assured her it was not. How can this one attack such a thing? she wondered. It will be like trying to attack a mountain!

Nevertheless, she had to try. Flapping up to gain height above the craft, she gathered herself, then dropped into a swift gliding dive and struck the hull of the ship with extended razor-sharp talons. Those talons could have cut a mammoth in two with a single blow, but to her dismay, they did not even scratch the ship's skin.

Within the ship, numerous instruments were evaluating and recording the Dragon's characteristics and activity. Motion images were made of her flight method, and still images were made of her internal organs and systems and skeleton. Her body weight, mass, and temperature were measured, and the size of her brain was evaluated. Intent upon their mining operation, The Industrious Ones paid no attention to any of this, inasmuch as the ship operated independently of them in all matters pertaining to itself.

The ship made a decision. It determined that the life form moving about it was nonintelligent and neither a danger to it nor a distraction to the mining operation. Accordingly, having sent all data on the Dragon into the biology records, the ship simply ignored Ko-ah-nag from then on. The vacuum beam continued to sweep back and forth across the ever-thinning expanse of rock that was the roof of the Trolls' cavern.

Ko-ah-nag realized that nothing she could do was going to affect the Sky Creature vessel in any way. She needed help, and there was only one source for it. She sent forth an agitated mind-touch message in all directions. *"This one is Ko-ah-nag, in the domain of the Trolls. A vessel of the Sky Creatures is here. It is somehow stealing the rock that is the roof of the Trolls' cavern. Soon the rock will all be gone. Sunlight will then fall upon the Trolls and they will all die! This one asks help/aid/assistance to prevent that. The Sky Creatures' vessel must be driven off, and only we of the Beautiful People can make an attack on it. But this one has tried and had no success by herself. It will take many of us—many. Come to this one's aid, my people!"*

Lithim, who was sprawled on the ground near the circle of logs, suddenly sat bolt upright, his eyes widening in surprise. Because Ko-ah-nag had sent her mind-touch plea out in a broad, general pattern, rather than directing it to a particular Dragon, the boy, to his astonishment, found himself receiving it. At the same moment, Gra-kwo arose from where he had been reclining and launched himself into the air, circling upward with powerful wing-beats that buffeted the nearby humans with forceful gusts of wind.

"Are you going to help, Gra-kwo?" Lithim called soundlessly with mind-touch. "Take care!'

"What is happening?" asked Mulng, alerted both by Lithim's actions and the sudden flight of the Dragon.

"There is a Sky Creature vessel over the Great Forest," Lithim explained. "Maybe it's the same one that was here. But somehow it's taking away the rock in the part of the forest where the Trolls live. If it takes it all, sun will shine into the Trolls' cavern! Gra-kwo and other Dragons are going there to try to drive the Sky Creatures away."

"May the Mother—and their own gods—be with them," Mulng muttered. He flashed a quick glance at the position of the sun. "There is nothing we can do to help until darkness falls and we can light the circle as Gurda in-structed. But that's still a long time off. I pray it won't come too late!"

Lithim's thoughts were on Gwolchmig and Kulglitch, whom he had come to know and like. They would be sleeping now, he knew, unaware of what was happening in the world above them, unaware of the terrible threat to their very existence. Was it really possible, the boy wondered, that the Sky Creatures could do as the Dragon Ko-ah-nag believed and make the stone roof of the Troll caverns, many thousands of paces wide and many hundreds of paces thick, just vanish? Remembering what the Foreseeing had shown, he knew that they indeed could, and he feared for the sleeping Trolls.

Gra-kwo sped over the plain with wings moving so fast they were nearly a blur. In only minutes from the time he had taken to the air, he was at the edge of the Great Forest. It unrolled beneath him like a vast, bumpy, dark-green carpet. In a little less than an hour, he was approaching the part of it that was the Troll domain. His sharp eyes could see that the sky in all directions was filled with many dark specks that were all moving, all converging upon the same part of the forest toward which he was headed. As he and they closed upon it, they became visible to him as winged forms of iridescent red, green, blue, brown, bronze, and silver. By the dozens, the Beautiful People were coming together in answer to Ko-ah-nag's plea. It was a sight that had never before been seen, for Dragons simply did not gather into crowds.

But now they had, and scores of winged forms were wheeling and circling about the gigantic, silver-gray, arrowhead-shaped vessel. Many had tried to attack it with their talons, as Ko-ah-nag had, but it quickly became obvious this was useless. A number of those that had come were mages, one of whom was the High Wizard Klo-gra-hwurg-ka-urgu-nga, who now took command. *"Our claws cannot scratch it,"* he told them all with mind-touch. *"Let us see if it will burn. Let those of us who are mages use the Spell of Breath of Flame."*

The mages, Gra-kwo among them, separated themselves from the others and swooped upon the vessel, emitting blasts of fire that exploded against its hull. Flapping upward, they glanced back to see what damage had been done by this initial attack.

There was none. The ship was unmarked, unscorched, as if the fire had never struck it.

But throughout the ship, instruments were again busy. They reported that the single creature that had been flying about the ship had been joined by many others and that some of these were emitting energy bursts of low-level intensity, which had struck the hull in a number of places. While no damage could be done to the ship in such fashion, it was obvious that the creatures were attempting to cause damage; and it was possible that they might have some other, more effective way, of doing so. The ship made a decision to eliminate any potential threat.

A pulse of radiant energy spread out in all directions from the ship, like a ripple caused by the dropping of a pebble into a still pool. Those Dragons nearest the ship, within a range of a mile or so, were instantly incinerated into puffs of ash. Those farther out burst into flame and went plummeting to earth like a score of blazing meteors. A very few, who were fortunate enough to be sufficiently far out, where the ripple of energy had begun to spread and dissipate, were merely badly scorched.

One of these was Gra-kwo, who had continued to climb after directing his Breath of Flame against the ship and was some three miles above it. A wave of searing heat washed through his body, and, with a shriek of agony, he began to fall, twisting and cartwheeling toward the forest below. But desperately, despite the pain, he managed to spread his wings and turn his plunge into an angling glide.

He landed hard at the very edge of the rocky area and the sand-covered ground out of which broken trees were poking up. His whole body throbbed with agony, but he was far more concerned about things other than his pain. Twisting his neck, he peered up at the sky. Except for the arrowhead shape of the Sky Creature vessel, sitting atop its slowly moving, swirling cone of rock dust, the sky was empty. There were no winged Dragon forms in sight.

Gra-kwo gave a wailing sigh of grief. He knew that, with the possible exception of a few others like himself, who had been far enough away from the burst of heat, all the Beautiful People who had come to drive the Sky Creatures away from the Great Forest were now dead, including his beloved old teacher, Klo-gra-hwurg-ka-urgu-nga. And fear squeezed at his heart, for he also knew that virtually all of the Northland Dragons had been here. The Beautiful People, the Dragons, were not a plentiful race like the humans. Because of their enormously long lives and their need for huge quantities of food, which required a vast hunting range for each Dragon, nature had seen to it that their numbers were kept low. Gra-kwo feared that, except for a few feeble elders and a few unhatched eggs, he might be the only Dragon left in this part of the world—perhaps in the entire world.

And even as this horrifying thought shivered in his mind, he was startled by a vast rumbling, clattering noise. Turning his head, he saw that the brown, swirling cone from the Sky Creature vessel had vanished. And so had the miles and miles of rocky surface that had been uncovered in the heart of the forest. The vacuum beam had finally sucked up the last of it except for a narrow ledge running around its entire perimeter, from which loose rocks were now sliding into the chasm below, causing the clattering sound.

With a new dread clutching at him, Gra-kwo struggled painfully to his feet and dragged himself forward a few dozen paces to the edge of the crater. With a silent prayer to the First Egg, he peered down into it.

Lithim had described to him the utter blackness of the underground caverns and the torchlit city of the Trolls. But there was no blackness now. Sunlight was reaching all the way to the cavern's rocky floor, and Gra-kwo could clearly see the Troll community spread out far beneath him. He could even look down into each separate dwelling, for of course it had never rained in the cavern, and so the enclosures in which the Trolls lived had no roofs. And thus there had been nothing at all to keep the sunlight from falling upon the slumbering Trolls.

Gra-kwo looked for a long time, but he saw absolutely no motion, no sign of life. Another wail of grief was torn from his throat, for he was sure that the great race of Trolls, thousands strong, had been wiped out. The Earth-doom was moving relentlessly upon the world.

His lip curled back in a snarl of hate, Gra-kwo looked up toward the vessel of the Sky Creatures. But it was gone. With their work finished and their profit assured, The Industrious Ones had departed from the desolation they had created.

11

Since Gra-kwo had vanished from sight, heading toward the Great Forest, Lithim had forced himself to keep from contacting the Dragon, fearing to disturb him at a time when he might be having to focus all his concentration on the attack against the Sky Creatures. But finally the boy could stand it no longer. He was filled with an inexplicable feeling of dread and a sense that Gra-kwo was in trouble, so he sent out a probe of mind-touch. "Gra-kwo, are you all right? What is happening?"

The answering mind-touch did not come right away, as it generally did; and when the Dragon finally answered, Lithim was shocked by the pain and grief he felt in Gra-kwo's thoughts.

"This one is still alive, Lith-im. But what has happened is dreadful/terrible/tragic beyond belief. This one fears there may no longer be any Trolls living on the

world. And this one fears that his own kind, the Beautiful People, have been given a mortal blow."

"What do you mean?" questioned Lithim, his mind recoiling in horror at what his friend's thoughts suggested.

"The cavern of the Trolls is now a great open chasm, filled with sunlight. There is no sign of life in it. And all the Beautiful People that were here, save this one and perhaps a few others—are dead."

Mulng and Natl were staring at Lithim with concern, for the boy had turned pale and his face wore an expression of horror. "The Trolls—the Trolls may all be dead," he told them in a choked voice. "And many Dragons are dead, too!"

"May the Mother receive them," whispered Natl, her face as horror-stricken as the boy's.

"Natl, I begin to fear that you and the others who thought we shouldn't depend upon Gurda's prophecy were right," said Mulng bitterly. "Because of it, we have no choice but to wait until darkness before we can do anything, and that may be too late—the world could be in ruins and all creatures dead by then!"

This was Lithim's thought, too. "There's no hope," he muttered. "We can't fight the Sky Things, Gurda's way or any other."

He had spoken aloud, but almost unconsciously he had directed his thoughts to Gra-kwo in mind-touch, and the Dragon responded. "No. There is hope. There is still hope for your kind, and for the Little People and the Alfar, and for all of the unthinking creatures that live on the world, from mammoths to mice! It is for all those that we must still carry out Gurda's instructions."

"But how can we, now?" Lithim questioned despairingly. "If—if most of the other Beautiful People are dead, as you fear, then how can we send the signal to light up all the wooden designs at the same time? There won't be any Dragons at most of the designs now, if they all flew off to the forest as you did, and were— were killed."

"Wait. This one will try to find out how things stand," Gra-kwo told him.

Still ignoring the pain of his scorched body, Gra-kwo sent out a mind-touch call to any other Dragons that might be alive to receive it. "This one is Gra-kwo, in the Great Forest. This one calls to all Beautiful People anywhere. Are there any receiving this one's thoughts?"

After a moment, to his joy, replies began to come to him.

"This one is Hoh-nig-ma. This one is in the Great Forest, too, but is badly hurt. This one cannot fly anymore."

"This one is Gon-klo-hoh-kah-an, on Purple Mountain. Why do you seek contact, Gra-kwo? This one senses great trouble."

"This one is Nah, on Silver-Tip Mountain."

"This one is Kah-on-gun-ag, in the land of the humans who ride upon the backs of horses. By the First Egg, what has happened?"

Only four, thought Gra-kwo with a spasm of grief, but he quickly thrust that aside and concentrated on how these four might be used to carry out the plan for setting flame to all the log constructions simultaneously. There was no problem in the land of the Horse People, for Kah-on-gun-ag was there, but there were now no Dragons in the territories of the Little People or at Soonchen, of course. And there were no Trolls to light the huge log square they had constructed in the clearing near the erstwhile entrance to their cavern.

"The attack on the Sky Creatures was a failure," he told those receiving his thoughts. *"This one grieves to tell that most of those who took part in it are dead, and some of them were ones who were to have given the signal to set flame to the great log constructions. Some of you must take their places."*

He then contacted each separately, first sending a thought of consolation to the badly injured Hoh-nig-ma, who could be of no help. Then he conferred with Kah-on-gun-ag, instructing him to stay where he was and carry out his duty as planned. Next, he addressed Nah.

Among Dragons, who lived for centuries, Nah was virtually a baby, having been hatched only eighteen years before. This was why he had not joined the other Dragons in the attack, considering himself too immature and useless, as Gra-kwo knew. *"Nah, young one, now you must carry out the task of one centuries older,"* he told the child. *"Fly to the territory of the Little People of the West. Go to the hill where they have erected their log shape. Tonight, when this one tells you, give the Little People the signal to set the shape afire."*

"This one goes, Gra-kwo."

With Gon-klo-hoh-kah-an, the situation was completely different, for he was probably the oldest of all the Beautiful People. Gra-kwo addressed him with great respect. *"Honored ancient one, are you still able to fly?"*

"A short distance perhaps, young Gra-kwo. Where do you wish this one to fly to?"

"To the territory of the Little People of the East, honored ancient one, to await my signal to tell them to set their construction afire."

"This one can make it that far. This one will do as you ask."

Finally, Gra-kwo reached out to his human friend. *"Lith-im, this one has seen to it that there will be Beautiful People where needed, with the Horse People and the Little People. This one will stay here and in honor of the Trolls will light their construction. This one will give the signal to all from here. You will have to be the 'Dragon' for the Soonchen Circle, my friend, and tell the other humans when to set it aflame."*

"All right, I'll do that," Lithim assured him. The boy turned to his father and Natl and explained things. "I guess all we can do is wait," he commented.

And so they continued to wait, as they had been doing, for night to fall. But it quickly became obvious that the wait would be far from boring. The crowd of people beside the log circle was brought surging to its feet in concern and fright by a blinding flash of white light that illuminated the northwestern portion of the sky, literally outshining the sun. It was instantly followed by a long, crackling rumble. The noise seemed to be far in the distance, but the ground shook noticeably. "In the Mother's name, what are they doing?" cried someone in the crowd, but no one could answer.

The flash, the noise, and the frightening quiver of the earth were repeated twice more as the afternoon wore toward evening. Then the crowd's attention was turned to another direction when someone noticed that a vast pall of dark smoke was lazily coiling into the sky at a point on the southwestern horizon. The crowd buzzed with speculation.

"The Earthdoom is moving about the land," said Natl grimly, her eyes on the smoke. "The Trolls are gone; the Dragons are nearly gone—what others may be gone before darkness arrives?"

Lithim sat with his chin resting on his knees, arms wrapped around his legs, wondering what the flashes of light and the noise and the smoke signified. What were the Sky Creatures doing to his world? How much of it would be left, even if Gurda's prophecy came true and the burning of the log constructions did cause the Sky Creatures to halt their destruction? As Natl had said, who else besides the Trolls and Dragons might be wiped out before morning came? The Alfar? The Little People? Humans? Will *I* still be alive tomorrow? he wondered.

From somewhere far off, there was a vast hissing sound. The crowd, which had grown largely silent, again began to squirm and murmur with fear and concern.

But the sun was definitely setting now. It was a red ball, no more than one fingerwidth above the horizon. The circle of logs was casting a single vast shadow that seemed to stretch for hundreds of paces across the plain, dwindling to a thin point.

Mulng stood up. "Twilight is gathering," he called in a loud voice. "Darkness is nearly here, praise be to the

Mother. Mages, take your places and await the signal. You others had best move back a distance, for when the logs blaze up, they will cast forth great heat, I think.''

With a ripple of motion, the crowd rose to its feet and began to flow away from the circle. Figures detached themselves from the crowd—the mages who had come to Soonchen moons ago from all over the Atlan Domain. All these men and women had witnessed the vision of the Earthdoom when they had cast their Spells of Foreseeing at the beginning of the year and had been stricken with despair when the High Chieftain of Atlan and the Daughters of the Mother had ordered them to ignore it. They had worked in secrecy to try to find some means of averting the threat that hung over the world, risking death by horrible execution if they were discovered, and then had braved the dangers of travel to get to Soonchen, where they could work together. They had faced the attack of the war band the High Chieftain had brought to Soonchen to wipe them out and had withstood the horror of the Magic of Darkness that the Chieftain's ally, the Alfar wizard Fengrim, had launched against them. Now all that was behind, and the final moment was at hand. Silently, they ranged themselves in a circle around the great ring of logs. Lithim stood beside his father, holding in his hand the big, curling horn of a forest ox, which he would blow when he received Gra-kwo's mind-touch, giving the signal that all could hear.

Darkness began to settle upon the plain.

Lithim found that his heart was beating faster. That seemed curious, for he was not actually facing any danger at the moment, but as he thought about it, he realized that he was intensely excited about the burning of the great log construction. What would happen when the huge ring of logs burst into flame? Would some unknown magic of Gurda's race explode into the sky, destroying the vessels of the invaders? Would they, too, burst into flames, like the logs? Or—and he cringed at the thought—would nothing happen at all? He was still not sure that he believed Gurda's prophecy would come true.

The darkness thickened. Stars became clearly visible in the sky.

In the Great Forest, Gra-kwo took flight, painfully flapping toward the great square construction the Trolls had erected. He circled over it for a moment, then went into a downward glide. He sent forth a single mind-touch command.

"Now!"

An instant later, gliding no more than half a wing's length above the logs, he commenced the Spell of Breath of Flame, directing spurts of fire at the logs over which he was passing. With a series of loud pops, one following another so rapidly it was almost a continuous sound, they caught fire.

As the command *"Now!"* snapped into his mind, Lithim raised the horn quickly to his lips and blew a sustained note. He had been practicing with the horn for some time, and the tone he produced was loud and clear, fully heard even by the mages farthest distant on the other side of the circle. Instantly, each mage cast a Spell of Fire at the circle, and with a single titanic *crack,* it exploded into flame. At the same moment, following signals from their Dragons, the mages of the Horse People and the Little People set their constructions burning.

Lithim, like all the other mages, fell back a distance from the blazing columns as the blast of heat from them began to beat at him. For a time he stared in fascination at the incredible sight of the wall of logs being consumed in writhing, twisting, snapping tongues of orange and yellow. Then he turned his attention upward, staring expectantly into the black, star-spangled sky. He did not know what he might see, but he expected some vast manifestation of power, some visible sign of the destruction of the Sky Creatures' vessels. He waited.

And waited. The sky remained unchanged. There were no bursts of light, no flashes, no sparkles, nothing to indicate that the Sky Creature vessels were being affected in any way.

"Nothing has happened!" Lithim exclaimed in a voice that was a shriek of protest.

But something *was* happening. On each of the ships of The Industrious Ones, instruments using the electronic mind-touch that was the creatures' form of communication were pouring a message into the mind of every crew member. "—ATTENTION—UNEXPLAINED-PHENOMENA-OCCURRING-ON-THE-PLANETARY-SURFACE-BELOW—."

Among those who responded to this information was the Representative of the Path. He tuned himself into his vessel's optical system, which was focused on the Earth's surface, covering an area that took in most of the northern half of the planet's eastern hemisphere. The instruments showed the surface in shades of color that indicated coolness and warmth, and the majority of the view was formed of dark to moderate blues, reflecting the coolness of the earth in springtime, after a long, cold winter. But in sharp, eye-catching contrast were patterns of bright, warm orange-yellow that formed distinct mathematical shapes: a circle, a square, and two triangles, close together in one place, with another circle far to the east and still another far, far, to the south. The Representative of the Path stared at this with astonishment for several seconds, then snapped a question at the ship. *"—how are these shapes being produced?—"*

"—THEY-ARE-FORMED-OF-SECTIONS-OF-PLANT-LIFE-CHIEFLY-OF-CELLULOSE-WHICH-IS-UNDER-GOING-OXIDATION—," the ship replied.

Instantly the Representative of the Path sent forth a mind-touch statement that was intended mainly for the Industrious One known as the Director, but that was received by all others on all the vessels. *"—this is the Representative of the Path—there is positive indication that intelligent life exists on the planet we are now processing—I order that all processing be terminated at once—now!—"*

12

The Industrious Ones had begun exploring the galaxy several thousand years before, and while they had found life forms on a number of the planets they had visited over the hundreds of centuries, they had found intelligent life—creatures that could *think*—on only a very few. It had become clear to them that intelligent life was quite rare in the universe, and some of them came to feel that intelligence was something very special and precious. A kind of religious philosophy known as the Way of the Path had come into being, with reverence for intelligent life as its basic principle. So when the Representative of the Path, who was a sort of priest–philosopher, had stated that intelligent life was present on Earth and ordered the stripping away of the planet's resources to stop, every Industrious One who was a follower of the Way of the Path awaited the order from the Director to halt all operations.

But the Industrious One who was the Director was not a follower of the Way of the Path; and he not only did not believe that intelligent life existed on the planet, he did not much care even if it did, for he did not intend to let the mere presence of intelligent life halt the highly profitable work that was being done. He also harbored a personal dislike for the Representative of the Path and was enraged by the Representative's action in demanding that the work be stopped. However, the Way of the Path had a great deal of power in The Industrious Ones' society, and the Director knew that if he simply disregarded the Representative's demand, he might well lose control of all the Followers of the Way on the five vessels, which would end all further work and halt all further profits. With open mind-touch so that all the rest of The Industrious Ones could "hear" him, he coldly challenged the Representative of the Path.

"—I dispute your action—the ship found no indication of intelligence with previous exhaustive investigation and even now does not positively indicate that these phenomena are intelligence-related—."

"—there can be no other interpretation—," stated the Representative of the Path. "—such perfect geometric shapes could only be produced by life forms with an understanding of mathematics—."

"—not true—," declared the Director. "—I myself have been on a world where nonintelligent arthropods constructed nests that were perfect pyramids—nonintelligent life forms can produce geometric shapes through instinct alone—."

"—the geometric forms on this planet are being oxi-

dized—I believe they were deliberately set afire to attract our attention—this indicates intelligence—," argued the Representative of the Path.

"—that is an unsubstantiated assumption—," charged the Director. *"—the oxidation could easily be from natural causes—fires are common in areas covered by certain types of plant life—."*

The Representative of the Path knew quite well that the Director was simply trying to sweep away the evidence of intelligent life on Earth because he did not want to stop the very profitable work that was being done. But the Representative had to be as careful in his dealings with the Director as the Director had to be with him. If he insisted that the work be permanently halted and the Director's objections were later found to be valid by the Examiners back on The Industrious Ones' home planet, the Director would be free to come back and do whatever he wished to this world.

"—I shall go down to the surface of the planet and locate some of the intelligent creatures to prove that they exist—," declared the Representative and broke mental contact with the Director.

He quickly made the necessary preparations for a planetary visit. Into the part of his body where the breathing apparatus was located he inserted an organic instrument that would enable him to temporarily breathe Earth's air. He then went to the part of the ship where the instruments for sending individuals outside were located, focused his mind into the ship's optical system, and regarded the glowing geometric shapes on the surface below.

"—I desire to journey to the planetary surface—," he told the ship. "—direct me to the illuminated circle at coordinates 95.3–124.8—."

A bubble of energy formed around him. An opening dilated in the ship's wall, and the bubble sped out into the darkness of Earth's night side, moving away from the ship, which still hung over the waters where Atlan Isle had been, and heading northeastward toward the coastline of the distant continent.

The Director was delighted to see his opponent depart. The highly efficient instruments of the ships had been so positive in ruling out the possibility of intelligent life on the little planet that the Director felt sure the Representative's search would be a failure. He thought that even if the Representative did succeed in finding some of the creatures that had made the burning geometric shapes, they would almost surely turn out to be no more than semi-intelligent and incapable of communication, like the arthropod pyramid builders he had mentioned to the Representative. Inasmuch as the ability to communicate was regarded as the prime example of intelligence, the Director felt sure that not even any Followers of the Path would be willing to put the welfare of such creatures ahead of the enormous profits that could come from the processing of the planet.

However, the Representative was the sort that might try to cause difficulties nonetheless, mused the Director. He decided it might be best if the Representative met with a fatal accident down on the planet's surface. The Director did not hesitate in the least at the prospect of murder, for the taking of the life of a rival or opponent, while very difficult to accomplish, was not considered a crime among The Industrious Ones.

The Director addressed the ship, using closed thought transference that could not be picked up by other Industrious Ones. *"—I desire to send an organic life-form simulating probe down to the planetary surface—,"* he told it. *"—provide examples of indigenous life forms—."*

It was common practice for survey vessels of The Industrious Ones to explore newly discovered planets by means of robotic creatures that resembled life forms of the planet and would thus not disrupt the ordinary life of the native animals and plants. The Director's ship was fully capable of carrying out the Director's wish, and it began to present three-dimensional holograms of Earth creatures for him to examine. Each hologram was accompanied by information on a creature's physical characteristics and capabilities.

"—hold—," ordered the Director when a hologram of a Dragon appeared. He considered the creature's makeup: gigantic size, capable of swift flight, excellent vision, well equipped with effective teeth and claws. Obviously it was a fierce predator, excellent for what he had in mind. *"—construct one of these—,"* he told the ship. *"—attune its brain to my thought emanations—."*

In the area of the ship where such things were done, construction of an artificial Dragon commenced. From storage areas, quantities of calcium, phosphate, and carbonate were brought together, and under the guidance of ship-directed machines, these elements and compounds were formed into a complete skeleton. From other storage areas came protoplasm, which was over-layed around the bones as tendons, muscles, nerve cells, and blood vessels. Heart, lungs, and several other organs were formed in place; but there was no stomach or digestive system, for the creature would gain the energy for living and moving from sunlight, moonlight, and starlight, gathered into it by means of special cells scattered throughout the body. Nor did it have a brain that was capable of anything other than instinctive impulses, for it would be controlled by the Director.

When the creature was finished, the ship notified the Director. He focused his mind on the Dragon and in moments was seeing through its eyes and controlling its movements. *"—allow exiting—,"* he ordered, and the floor of the ship in front of the Dragon dilated open. Under the Director's control, the Dragon launched itself out of the opening and began to glide down toward the Earth's surface in great spirals, heading in the same direction as that taken by the energy bubble in which the Representative of the Path was enclosed.

At the moment when the Representative of the Path left his ship, every pair of eyes in the crowd of people at the flaming circle of logs near Soonchen was fixed upon the sky. Like Lithim, everyone was desperately seeking some sign of the destruction of the Sky Creature vessels, but like Lithim, most everyone had just about given up hope.

"We don't know for sure what is supposed to happen," Mulng pointed out. "Gurda said nothing about the Sky Creatures being destroyed. Perhaps they will simply be driven off. Perhaps they are gone already."

"You are hoping against hope," Natl told him in a listless voice. "No magic has taken place; you know that. This thing is just a big bonfire in the shape of a ring. It can't do anything to make the Sky Creatures leave."

"What is that?" someone called suddenly. "There is a star moving in the sky!"

"Where?" questioned half a dozen voices. "I see it, too," someone else shouted. "Look to the west, low in the sky."

Every head turned. A bright point of light, like a large star, was speeding down out of the sky.

"By the Mother, it looks as if it is coming straight toward *us,*" said a voice near Lithim, which he recognized as that of Leng, the Chieftain of Soonchen village. He's right, thought the boy, with excitement beginning to tingle in his body. It *is* coming straight toward us. Perhaps something *is* happening!

As the point of light grew in size and brightness, a number of people began to move back, away from the burning circle. "They are coming to punish us," yelled someone, and the withdrawal became a panic-stricken flight in all directions into the darkness. Only the warriors and most of the mages remained, almost automatically moving toward one another to form a tight cluster of tense figures. But even many of these lost their nerve and broke into flight as the bright object continued to rush in seeming anger toward them, rapidly growing larger. At last, only Lithim, Mulng, Natl, the Alfar sorceress Alglinnadorn, and two or three other mages and a handful of warriors were left. They stood half crouched, as if ready themselves to flee, as the globe of light came to an abrupt stop with the apex of its bottom curve resting on the grass no more than a dozen paces from them. It was a dazzling, mottled bluish white, equal in height and width to the height of a tall human.

Something emerged from it and stood, apparently looking at them. There was an involuntary gasp from the humans as they realized they were actually seeing one of the dreaded Sky Creatures.

Lithim could see it fairly clearly in both the glow from the flaming circle of logs and the illumination of the shining globe, but he could not understand what sort of creature it was, for he had never seen anything remotely like it. It was about as big as he, a dull brownish black in color, with an oddly pocked and pitted appearance. He could not see anything on it that resembled a mouth, nose, or eyes; and indeed, it did not even seem to have a head. It was faintly insectlike, perhaps because it had a number of long, slim appendages that were apparently arms and legs, but more than anything it seemed to Lithim like a creature that was formed out of burned sticks of wood.

As he stared at it, something was suddenly streaming through his mind like a kind of continuous silent shout—
"ISEEKTHOSEOFINTELLIGENCETHOSEWHOCON-STRUCTEDTHEGEOMETRICPATTERNSTHOSEWHO FOLLOWTHEWAYOFTHEPATHAREYOUOFTHOSE—."
He realized that it was a form of mind-touch, but the flow of thoughts was so rapid he could not grasp their

meaning. It was obvious that they were coming from the creature and that it was trying to communicate. Uncertainly he sent his mind out toward it. "Slower, please! You are thinking too fast."

Instantly the thought flow coursing through his brain cut off. After a moment he felt mind-touch again, but now deliberately and carefully controlled and held back. "—you can communicate—you have intelligence—are you the builder of the burning circle?—"

"Well, one of them," Lithim told it, marveling that it communicated exactly as Dragons did. "I can talk to it," he reported to his father and the others around him, who were staring in apprehension at the strange creature. "It uses mind-touch, just like Dragons."

"Wonderful!" Mulng exclaimed. "Ask it what it wants, Lith. Ask it why is destroying our world!"

Lithim complied. "Why have you come to our world? Why are you destroying it?"

"—your planet holds vast resources—," the Representative told him. "—it is great profit to us to harvest and process them—but the Way of the Path admonishes us not to take profit from a world that supports intelligent life—once the other Industrious Ones know for sure of your existence the operations here will be permanently terminated—."

Lithim was puzzled by much of the Sky Creature's reply. The boy simply did not know the meaning of the term *profit* and did not understand the Representative's reference to the Way of the Path. But he did gather that the creature intended to tell others of its kind that there were thinking beings on the Earth and that this would permanently end the destruction.

"I don't understand everything," Lithim said to those around him. "But I think he is saying that if he tells the other Sky Creatures about us—that we can *think*—they won't do any more damage. He seems to be friendly."

There were exultant exclamations from some of the mages. "Thanks be to the Mother," said Mulng fervently. "And thanks be to Gurda. Somehow, these things she told us to build and set afire have made this happen."

Lithim sensed that everyone was relaxing, their fear of the Sky Creature evaporating as they understood that it was not only of no danger to them but was actually going to help end the danger to the entire world. He, too, felt the beginning of a great sense of relief. The world had been hurt, yes, but the worst of the Earthdoom was going to be averted.

Then he became aware of a rushing sound coming from above and growing in intensity. Jerking his head upward, he saw that a portion of the starlit sky was blotted out by a vast shape slicing down out of the darkness. In a flush of horror, he realized that the Sky Creature standing before him was about to be slain by the terrible claws of a swooping Dragon.

13

In the moments before the Dragon struck, a lightning bolt of thoughts coursed through Lithim's mind. The Sky Creature had indicated that it could probably halt the Earthdoom by communicating with the other Sky Creatures, but if it were killed now by the Dragon, the others would surely continue the world's destruction. Therefore, this Sky Creature had to be saved. But there was no way to stop the Dragon's swift plummet, no time to even "shout" at it with mind-touch, and Lithim didn't know if it would pay any attention to him even if he did try to communicate with it. He did the only thing he could think of, which was to activate a Spell of Illusion.

It was what was known among mages as a Dazzle Spell, to confuse a would-be attacker. Where the spindly Sky Creature had stood alone, there was suddenly a milling crowd of identical Sky Creatures, with the original and real one lost somewhere among them. Looking through the eyes of the artificial Dragon, the Director of the Industrious Ones was dumbfounded to see his intended prey abruptly explode into a dozen moving images of itself. Instinctively, the Dragon clutched at one of them, but its claws closed on empty air. An instant later, still acting on its instincts, the Dragon gave a powerful beat of its wings and began ascending skyward so it would not strike the ground.

Lithim and the others standing close to him were staggered by the snap of wind from the great wings, and the Sky Creature went skittering backward in a series of odd, jerky motions, as if trying to hold its balance. Peering up at the vast shape of the Dragon silhouetted against the starlit sky, Lithim sent out a desperate mind-touch call. "Stop!" he pleaded. "I don't know who you are, but you must not attack this Sky Creature. It isn't an enemy, it is—" He broke off abruptly, for he had become aware that his thoughts were literally flowing into emptiness. There was nothing receiving them where the Dragon's mind should be. With a shock, the boy realized that the Dragon was mindless; but he sensed the presence of a mind, far distant, controlling the creature.

Puzzled by the inexplicable appearance of a whole crowd of identical Representatives of the Path, and angered at the disruption of his plan to eliminate the Representative, the Director caused the Dragon to wheel about and once again prepare to launch itself into a dive. He realized that most of the figures of the Representative must be illusionary images, and he reasoned that one of them had to be the real one. He intended

125

to make the Dragon simply flail away with its claws until it caught the living being, and then he would have the Dragon crush out the Representative's life. It was difficult to kill an Industrious One, but the Director felt sure that the Dragon could do it.

"It's going to attack again," said Mulng, who, like Lithim, was staring up into the sky, tracking the Dragon's flight as its huge body blotted out the stars behind it. "Tell it to stop, Lith!"

"There's something wrong with it," Lithim told him in a voice that throbbed with desperation. "I can't feel any thoughts when I try to mind-touch it."

"We have to stop it somehow," said Mulng, his face twisted with anxiety. "Your Dazzle Spell will wear off in a few moments."

At that instant, unexpected help arrived. As soon as he had finished setting aflame the great square that the Trolls had erected, Gra-kwo started out to fly back to be with his friend Lithim for whatever more might happen on this night of the Earthdoom. His progress was slow because of the pain in his scorched body, but eventually he saw the glow of the burning Soonchen Circle ahead of him; and as he grew nearer, he became aware of a swirl of excited, frightened, desperate human thoughts. *"Lith-im, what is happening?"* he questioned with mind-touch.

"Gra-kwo! A Sky Creature is here and it wants to help us, but there's a Dragon trying to attack it! Can you make the Dragon stop?"

With the keen vision of a nocturnal predator, Gra-kwo quickly located the other Dragon just as it was dropping into a swoop. As Lithim had done, Gra-kwo tried to communicate with it and instantly discovered its mindlessness. He did not understand what the creature was, but he knew that it was not truly one of the Beautiful People, so he had no compunction about killing it. Vigorously beating his wings, he raced to intercept it.

The Director suddenly became aware of the vast winged form rushing at his robot and realized that it meant to attack. Cursing himself for not having thought to have some type of energy weapon built into the robot's body, he sought to guide it to escape. If he could make the real Dragon follow the robot, he reasoned, and lure it into the range of his spacecraft's weapons, he could destroy it and then bring the robot back to finish off the Representative of the Path.

But the Director had paid no attention to the Dragons' attack on the Industrious Ones' vessel above the cavern of the Trolls, so he did not know that some Dragons were capable of belching blasts of fire from their mouths. He was astounded, therefore, when a fiery stream struck the robot's body as Gra-kwo performed the Spell of Breath of Flame. The blast damaged the robot's eyes and shriveled one of its wings, and the Director found that he could no longer control it. It was falling headlong toward the ground, and the Director pulled his mind free of it before it struck.

The robot Dragon smashed into the ground no more than a hundred yards from the cluster of humans and the Representative of the Path. Gra-kwo came gliding down to land near it.

"—what has taken place?—" questioned the Representative's mind-touch. "—I do not understand the significance of these events—."

Gra-kwo, as well as Lithim, had received this query, and it was the Dragon who answered. "That creature was attempting to kill/destroy/eradicate you," he told the Representative. "This one has prevented that." Like Lithim, he was amazed that the Sky Creature communicated in the same way as Dragons.

"—why was the creature seeking to destroy me?—" the Representative of the Path asked. "—was it needing sustenance?—"

Lithim felt sure that the strange Dragon had not been attacking out of hunger. "No," he told the Sky Creature. "There was something wrong with it. It did not appear to be thinking for itself. I had the feeling that something somewhere else was controlling it."

At this comment, the Sky Creature seemed to freeze into immobility, and Lithim worriedly wondered if something was the matter with it. Actually, startled by what the boy had just told him, the Representative was examining the body of the Dragon robot with a number of his senses. In moments, he completely understood all that had taken place. Industrious Ones were capable of anger, and the Representative felt a cold fury that the Director had the insolence to try to murder him. He reached out with open mind-touch to all The Industrious Ones on the five vessels hanging in Earth's sky.

"—I am on the surface of the planet—to prevent me from proving the existence of intelligent life here, the Director attempted to have me destroyed by means of a construct of a planetary predator created by his vessel—but I was saved from destruction by some of the intelligent life forms that reside here—thus the proof has been established and I demand that the processing of this planet be instantly terminated—."

"—heed me, Industrious Ones—," came the open mind-touch of the Director. "—I sought to eliminate the Representative of the Path because I foresaw that he would do precisely as he is doing—he is seeking to terminate our work and bring an end to all our profits with a pretense that there is true intelligent life on the planet—but whatever creatures he has found are not truly intelligent—the instruments of our vessels have indicated no signs of true intelligence anywhere on the planet—no artificial energy emanations of any sort were detected—."

"—nevertheless, there is intelligent life here—," insisted the Representative of the Path. "—there are creatures capable of rational thought—."

"—prove this—," demanded the Director, feeling sure there was no way the Representative could actually do so.

"—very well—," returned the Representative, satisfaction clear in his thought. "—I will ask one of them to communicate with you all, mind to mind, so that you may judge for yourselves—."

He contacted Lithim, using the form of mind-touch that only the boy would receive. "—creature—," he communicated, "—all The Industrious Ones are now awaiting communication from you—make them under-

stand that you are capable of intelligent thought and your world will be saved—."

Lithim was thunderstruck. He licked his lips nervously, staring at the Sky Creature uncertainly. It's all up to me, he thought. It's *me* who must save the world! But what if I do something wrong? What if they don't understand me? What if I can't even reach them for some reason?

Then, abruptly, a memory of the night of the Mage Council, many moons before, swam into his thoughts. It was the night when Mulng had agreed to let him go with the Trolls on the journey to contact Gurda. Mulng had made that decision because of the words of Neomah, the mage of the Little People. Speaking of Lithim, she had said, "He still has a great part to play in averting the Earthdoom." If Neomah was right, thought Lithim, then *this* is the moment when I must play that part. Everything else has led up to *this*. I must simply do the best that I can.

Taking a deep breath, he reached out with mindtouch, letting it stream toward the vastness of the sky and the waiting Sky Creatures. "I speak to you in the name of all the thinking creatures of this world, and I beg you not to destroy our home. You are much stronger and more powerful than we are, so you can do whatever you wish. You have the power to let us live or make us die. Please—let us live."

Every Industrious One in the five vessels received and understood his message. There was no doubt at all but that it was the message of a rational, thinking being. The Director, astounded by this rebuttal of his beliefs, felt the thoughts of the other Industrious Ones begin to swirl through his mind—"—*terminate the processing—halt the processing—terminate the operations—.*" At first the demands were only from those who were Followers of the Path, but it quickly became obvious that many others were joining in. There was no dissent. The Director realized that he was beaten.

"—*terminate all operations on the planet—,*" he ordered. At once, energy beams were turned off; probing devices were deactivated; the breakdown of minerals, liquids, and gases was halted. As Gurda had predicted, the Earthdoom came to a stop.

"—*it is done—,*" said the Representative of the Path in Lithim's mind. "—*the processing of your planet has been halted—we shall shortly depart—may you continue to Follow the Path in security—.*"

With odd, sidling steps, he moved backward into the energy bubble and vanished into it. Instantly it went rushing off like a thrown pebble, swiftly dwindling in size until it was no more than a star-sized point of light ascending into the sky.

"What has happened?" Natl cried out. "Where is the Sky Creature going?"

"They're leaving," said Lithim slowly. "All of them. It's all over. They have stopped the Earthdoom. The world is safe."

She and his father stared at him, their faces beginning to register joy. Lithim realized that he could make out these expressions because there was a faint light suffusing everything. It was that time of morning just before the first red edge of the sun becomes visible over the rim of the world, and this was the pale gray light that preceded the pink flush of dawn.

This would be the first dawn in almost a year in which the threat of the Earthdoom did not lie upon the world, thought Lithim, wonderingly. It's all over, he told himself. It's *really* all over. The world has been saved—and *I* helped to save it!

Epilogue

On a late afternoon two years after the Night of the Fiery Circle, Lithim, Mulng, and Natl stood on the wall of Soonchen and watched the sun set. It was a fiery sunset that had painted the western sky a brilliant mottled red.

"The sunsets have been much redder than they were in the days before the Sky Creatures came," murmured the boy. "I wonder if something the Sky Creatures did caused this?"

"Perhaps," said Mulng. "Mother knows, the Sky Creatures did many things that have changed our world." There was bitterness in his voice.

Lithim nodded. It was, indeed, a much different world from what it had been before the Sky Creatures came. The Trolls were gone, as if they had never existed, and the Dragons were dying out; within a few centuries, those still left would be gone. They will both become nothing more than legends, thought Lithim sadly. Many humans were frankly little concerned by the extinction of the Trolls, for Trolls and humans had been bitter, warring enemies before the threat of the Earthdoom had made them allies. But Lithim and his father had come to know and respect the Trolls, and felt that the extermination of their culture was a loss for the world. And as for the Dragons, even though he would not be alive to witness their ending, the knowledge that the world would someday be without these huge, beautiful creatures was a grief to Lithim.

The human race, too, had been injured by the actions of the Sky Creatures. In the days following the Night of the Fiery Circle, the people of Soonchen had rejoiced that the Earthdoom had been stopped before it could do any of the terrible damage that had been shown to mages in the Foreseeing. But as time went on, they began to learn that serious damage *had* been done. From wanderers, they heard of the destruction of Atlan Isle. They also learned, in time, of other human communities that had been destroyed, with great loss of life. Two villages on the seacoast had been inundated by a tidal wave, and an inland community had been decimated by an earthquake, both of these things caused by the activity of the Sky Creatures.

With the loss of its capital, Atlan Dis, and an end to the flow of traders between the capital and the mainland villages, the Atlan Domain had dissolved. Each village had been thrown on its own, and as time went on, there was less and less communication between them, and finally, none at all. Most of the villages had been deserted, the people leaving them to live in caves, where they felt safe from the open sky out of which the terror of the Sky Creatures had come. There was talk of this in Soonchen, too. We will become cave people, thought Lithim with sorrow, for he realized that the civilization that had existed for centuries was collapsing.

But worse even than this, for Lithim and the other mages, was the dreadful knowledge that something the Sky Creatures had done had altered the world in a special way. The magic had stopped.

It was not entirely gone, for Lithim and all the adult mages could still cast spells, as they always had. But some of the last communications from other villages, as well as word from the Little People, with whom Mulng had kept in touch, indicated that of all the children born since the night the Sky Creatures had departed, not one had the slightest bit of mage power. It seemed shockingly clear that some activity of the Sky Creatures had wiped out the potential for magic in the world. With no more mages being born, what had been an Age of Magic was drawing to a close.

Thus, even though the Earthdoom had been averted, the coming of the Sky Creatures had left deep scars on the world. Some of those, such as the huge chasm in the Great Forest, the earth could repair, covering them over, in time, with new soil and plant growth. But the earth could never replace what had been taken from it. It could never again produce a creature such as a Troll or Dragon, and Lithim suspected that it might never again produce an Age of Magic.

He drew in a deep breath and let it out in a plaintive

sigh. Well, he thought, the world was saved at great cost, but at least it *was* saved.

However, something was nagging at his mind. "Do you think it could ever happen again?" he wondered. "Another Earthdoom?"

"If it happened once, it could happen again," Natl asserted.

Mulng nodded. "I do not think the Sky Creatures will ever come back," he said, "but there may be other things like them in the realms beyond the stars. For that matter, there might even be some right here on this world, like Fengrim, who would seek to do such a thing if they could because they felt they would gain from it."

"If the magic is gone and there are no more mages, who will foresee another Earthdoom and warn against it?" Lithim asked in a low voice. "Who would be able to fight it as we did?"

Neither the man nor the woman answered him for a moment. Then Mulng said, "There may be ways other than magic. Ways such as the Sky Creatures had. In the future, without magic, people may learn such ways and use them to warn of another Earthdoom and to fight it. There will always be mages of some kind, I think."

Lithim swiveled his head slowly to take in the panorama that lay beyond the wall. Beneath the vivid sky, the plain that stretched toward the rolling, hilly country of the Little People was an ocean of orange, with the distant Darkwood Forest a shaggy purple shadow squatting upon it. The little lake, at the edge of which the village sat, mirrored the red sky with its bright surface.

"We almost lost this," said Lithim soberly, making a

sweep of his arm to indicate the blaze of color. "I pray that it may never be threatened again. But if the world ever does face another Earthdoom, I hope that the mages of that time will be able to fight it, whether they use magic or something else. I hope that *they* will be listened to and believed—as we were not! I hope they will not have to struggle against the stupidity of such as the High Chieftain and the Daughters of the Mother. I pray that they will be able to keep from losing *their* world!"

From the lake floated the sonorous sounds of honking geese. Far out upon the plain, a wolf howl began to moan. Somewhere in the village, a small child gave a high-pitched shriek of laughter. The creatures of the earth were carrying on with their lives in a clean, unthreatened, beautiful world.

About the Author

TOM MCGOWEN is the author of nearly forty books for young people. He is the recipient of the Children's Reading Round Table of Chicago award for Outstanding Contributions to the Field of Children's Literature. His books include *The Magician's Apprentice, The Magician's Company,* and *The Magicians' Challenge,* as well as two previous books in the Age of Magic trilogy: *The Magical Fellowship* and *A Trial of Magic.*

Mr. McGowen and his wife live in Norridge, Illinois. They have four children and eleven grandchildren.

FIC
MCG

McGowen, Tom.

A question of magic.